Famous German Novellas
of the 19ᵗʰ Century

Famous German Novellas

of the 19th Century

Theodor Storm: Immensee
Translated by C. W. Bell

Adelbert von Chamisso: Peter Schlemihl
Translated by Henry Morley

Adalbert Stifter: Brigitta
Translated by Edward Fitzgerald

MONDIAL

Famous German Novellas of the 19ᵗʰ Century
(Theodor Storm: Immensee; Adelbert von Chamisso:
Peter Schlemihl; Adalbert Stifter: Brigitta)
Translated by C. W. Bell, Henry Morley, Edward
Fitzgerald
© Mondial, New York, 2005
www.mondialbooks.com
ISBN 1-59569-014-X

Theodor W. Storm

Immensee

The Old Man

One afternoon in the late autumn a well-dressed old man was
walking slowly down the street. He appeared to be returning
home from a walk, for his buckle-shoes, which followed a
fashion long since out of date, were covered with dust.

Under his arm he carried a long, gold-headed cane; his
dark eyes, in which the whole of his long-lost youth seemed
to have centred, and which contrasted strangely with his
snow-white hair, gazed calmly on the sights around him or
peered into the town below as it lay before him, bathed in the
haze of sunset. He appeared to be almost a stranger, for of
the passers-by only a few greeted him, although many a one
involuntarily was compelled to gaze into those grave eyes.

At last he halted before a high, gabled house, cast one
more glance out toward the town, and then passed into the
hall. At the sound of the door-bell some one in the room within drew aside the green curtain from a small window that
looked out on to the hall, and the face of an old woman was
seen behind it. The man made a sign to her with his cane.

"No light yet!" he said in a slightly southern accent, and
the housekeeper let the curtain fall again.

The old man now passed through the broad hall, through
an inner hall, wherein against the walls stood huge oaken
chests bearing porcelain vases; then through the door opposite he entered a small lobby, from which a narrow staircase
led to the upper rooms at the back of the house. He climbed
the stairs slowly, unlocked a door at the top, and landed in a
room of medium size.

It was a comfortable, quiet retreat. One of the walls was lined with cupboards and bookcases; on the other hung pictures of men and places; on a table with a green cover lay a number of open books, and before the table stood a massive arm-chair with a red velvet cushion.

After the old man had placed his hat and stick in a corner, he sat down in the arm-chair and, folding his hands, seemed to be taking his rest after his walk. While he sat thus, it was growing gradually darker; and before long a moonbeam came streaming through the window-panes and upon the pictures on the wall; and as the bright band of light passed slowly onward the old man followed it involuntarily with his eyes.

Now it reached a little picture in a simple black frame. "Elisabeth!" said the old man softly; and as he uttered the word, time had changed: *he was young again.*

The Children

Before very long the dainty form of a little maiden advanced toward him. Her name was Elisabeth, and she might have been five years old. He himself was twice that age. Round her neck she wore a red silk kerchief which was very becoming to her brown eyes.

"Reinhard!" she cried, "we have a holiday, a holiday! No school the whole day and none to-morrow either!"

Reinhard was carrying his slate under his arm, but he flung it behind the front door, and then both the children ran through the house into the garden and through the garden gate out into the meadow. The unexpected holiday came to them at a most happily opportune moment.

It was in the meadow that Reinhard, with Elisabeth's help, had built a house out of sods of grass. They meant to live in it during the summer evenings; but it still wanted a bench. He set to work at once; nails, hammer, and the necessary boards were already to hand.

While he was thus engaged, Elisabeth went along the dyke, gathering the ring-shaped seeds of the wild mallow in her apron, with the object of making herself chains and necklaces out of them; so that when Reinhard had at last finished his bench in spite of many a crookedly hammered nail, and came out into the sunlight again, she was already wandering far away at the other end of the meadow.

"Elisabeth!" he called, "Elisabeth!" and then she came, her hair streaming behind her.

"Come here," he said; "our house is finished now. Why, you have got quite hot! Come in, and let us sit on the new bench. I will tell you a story."

So they both went in and sat down on the new bench. Elisabeth took the little seed-rings out of her apron and strung them on long threads. Reinhard began his tale: "There were once upon a time three spinning-women..." *

"Oh!" said Elisabeth, "I know that off by heart; you really must not always tell me the same story."

Accordingly Reinhard had to give up the story of the three spinning-women and tell instead the story of the poor man who was cast into the den of lions.

"It was now night," he said, "black night, you know, and the lions were asleep. But every now and then they would yawn in their sleep and shoot out their red tongues. And then the man would shudder and think it was morning. All at once a bright light fell all about him, and when he looked up an angel was standing before him. The angel beckoned to him with his hand and then went straight into the rocks."

Elisabeth had been listening attentively. "An angel?" she said. "Had he wings then?"

"It is only a story," answered Reinhard; "there are no angels, you know."

"Oh, fie! Reinhard!" she said, staring him straight in the face.

He looked at her with a frown, and she asked him hesitatingly: "Well, why do they always say there are? mother, and aunt, and at school as well?"

"I don't know," he answered.

"But tell me," said Elisabeth, "are there no lions either?"

"Lions? Are there lions? In India, yes. The heathen priests harness them to their carriages, and drive about the

desert with them. When I'm big, I mean to go out there myself. It is thousands of times more beautiful in that country
than it is here at home; there's no winter at all there. And you
must come with me. Will you?"

"Yes," said Elisabeth; "but mother must come with us,
and your mother as well."

"No," said Reinhard, "they will be too old then, and cannot come with us."

"But I mayn't go by myself."

"Oh, but you may right enough; you will then really be
my wife, and the others will have no say in the matter."

"But mother will cry!"

"We shall come back again of course," said Reinhard impetuously. "Now just tell me straight out, will you go with
me? If not, I will go all alone, and then I shall never come
back again."

The little girl came very near to crying. "Please don't
look so angry," said she; "I will go to India with you."

Reinhard seized both her hands with frantic glee, and
rushed out with her into the meadow.

"To India, to India!" he sang, and swung her round and
round, so that her little red kerchief was whirled from off
her neck. Then he suddenly let her go and said solemnly:

"Nothing will come of it, I'm sure; you haven't the pluck."

"Elisabeth! Reinhard!" some one was now calling from
the garden gate. "Here we are!" the children answered, and
raced home hand in hand.

In the Woods

So the children lived together. She was often too quiet for
him, and he was often too head-strong for her, but for all that
they stuck to one another. They spent nearly all their leisure
hours together: in winter in their mothers' tiny rooms, during the summer in wood and field.

Once when Elisabeth was scolded by the teacher in Reinhard's hearing, he angrily banged his slate upon the table

in order to turn upon himself the master's wrath. This failed to attract attention.

But Reinhard paid no further attention to the geography lessons, and instead he composed a long poem, in which he compared himself to a young eagle, the schoolmaster to a grey crow, and Elisabeth to a white dove; the eagle vowed vengeance on the grey crow, as soon as his wings had grown.

Tears stood in the young poet's eyes: he felt very proud of himself. When he reached home he contrived to get hold of a little parchment-bound volume with a lot of blank pages in it; and on the first pages he elaborately wrote out his first poem.

Soon after this he went to another school. Here he made many new friendships among boys of his own age, but this did not interrupt his comings and goings with Elisabeth. Of the stories which he had formerly told her over and over again he now began to write down the ones which she had liked best, and in doing so the fancy often took him to weave in something of his own thoughts; yet, for some reason he could not understand, he could never manage it.

So he wrote them down exactly as he had heard them himself. Then he handed them over to Elisabeth, who kept them carefully in a drawer of her writing-desk, and now and again of an evening when he was present it afforded him agreeable satisfaction to hear her reading aloud to her mother these little tales out of the notebooks in which he had written them.

Seven years had gone by. Reinhard was to leave the town in order to proceed to his higher education. Elisabeth could not bring herself to think that there would now be a time to be passed entirely without Reinhard. She was delighted when he told her one day that he would continue to write out stories for her as before; he would send them to her in the letters to his mother, and then she would have to write back to him and tell him how she liked them.

The day of departure was approaching, but ere it came a good deal more poetry found its way into the parchment-bound volume. This was the one secret he kept from Elisabeth, although she herself had inspired the whole book and most of the songs, which gradually had filled up almost half of the blank pages.

It was the month of June, and Reinhard was to start on the following day. It was proposed to spend one more festive day together and therefore a picnic was arranged for a rather large party of friends in an adjacent forest.

It was an hour's drive along the road to the edge of the wood, and there the company took down the provision baskets from the carriages and walked the rest of the way. The road lay first of all through a pine grove, where it was cool and darksome, and the ground was all strewed with pine needles.

After half an hour's walk they passed out of the gloom of the pine trees into a bright fresh beech wood. Here everything was light and green; every here and there a sunbeam burst through the leafy branches, and high above their heads a squirrel was leaping from branch to branch.

The party came to a halt at a certain spot, over which the topmost branches of ancient beech trees interwove a transparent canopy of leaves. Elisabeth's mother opened one of the baskets, and an old gentleman constituted himself quartermaster.

"Round me, all of you young people," he cried, "and attend carefully to what I have to say to you. For lunch each one of you will now get two dry rolls; the butter has been left behind at home. The extras every one must find for himself. There are plenty of strawberries in the wood—that is, for anyone who knows where to find them. Unless you are sharp, you'll have to eat dry bread; that's the way of the world all over. Do you understand what I say?"

"Yes, yes," cried the young folks.

"Yes, but look here," said the old gentleman, "I have not done yet. We old folks have done enough roaming about in our time, and therefore we will stay at home now, here, I mean, under these wide-spreading trees, and we'll peel the potatoes and make a fire and lay the table, and by twelve o'clock the eggs shall be boiled.

"In return for all this you will be owing us half of your strawberries, so that we may also be able to serve some dessert. So off you go now, east and west, and mind be honest."

The young folks cast many a roguish glance at one another.

"Wait," cried the old gentleman once again. "I suppose I need not tell you this, that whoever finds none need not produce any; but take particular note of this, that he will get nothing out of us old folks either. Now you have had enough good advice for to-day; and if you gather strawberries to match you will get on very well for the present at any rate."

The young people were of the same opinion, and pairing off in couples set out on their quest.

"Come along, Elisabeth," said Reinhard, "I know where there is a clump of strawberry bushes; you shan't eat dry bread."

Elisabeth tied the green ribbons of her straw hat together and hung it on her arm. "Come on, then," she said, "the basket is ready."

Off into the wood they went, on and on; on through moist shady glens, where everything was so peaceful, except for the cry of the falcon flying unseen in the heavens far above their heads; on again through the thick brushwood, so thick that Reinhard must needs go on ahead to make a track, here snapping off a branch, there bending aside a trailing vine. But ere long he heard Elisabeth behind him calling out his name. He turned round.

"Reinhard!" she called, "do wait for me! Reinhard!"

He could not see her, but at length he caught sight of her some way off struggling with the undergrowth, her dainty head just peeping out over the tops of the ferns. So back he went once more and brought her out from the tangled mass of briar and brake into an open space where blue butterflies fluttered among the solitary wood blossoms.

Reinhard brushed the damp hair away from her heated face, and would have tied the straw hat upon her head, but she refused; yet at his earnest request she consented after all.

"But where are your strawberries?" she asked at length, standing still and drawing a deep breath.

"They were here," he said, "but the toads have got here before us, or the martens, or perhaps the fairies."

"Yes," said Elisabeth, "the leaves are still here; but not a word about fairies in this place. Come along, I'm not a bit tired yet; let us look farther on."

In front of them ran a little brook, and on the far side the wood began again. Reinhard raised Elisabeth in his arms and carried her over. After a while they emerged from the shady foliage and stood in a wide clearing.

"There must be strawberries here," said the girl, "it all smells so sweet."

They searched about the sunny spot, but they found none. "No," said Reinhard, "it is only the smell of the heather."

Everywhere was a confusion of raspberry-bushes and holly, and the air was filled with a strong smell of heather, patches of which alternated with the short grass over these open spaces.

"How lonely it is here!" said Elisabeth "I wonder where the others are?"

Reinhard had never thought of getting back.

"Wait a bit," he said, holding his hand aloft; "where is the wind coming from?" But wind there was none.

"Listen!" said Elisabeth, "I think I heard them talking. Just give a call in that direction."

Reinhard hollowed his hand and shouted: "Come here!"

"Here!" was echoed back.

"They answered," cried Elisabeth clapping her hands.

"No, that was nothing; it was only the echo."

Elisabeth seized Reinhard's hand. "I'm frightened!" she said.

"Oh! no, you must not be frightened. It is lovely here. Sit down there in the shade among the long grass. Let us rest awhile: we'll find the others soon enough."

Elisabeth sat down under the overhanging branch of a beech and listened intently in every direction. Reinhard sat a few paces off on a tree stump, and gazed over at her in silence.

The sun was just above their heads, shining with the full glare of midday heat. Tiny, gold-flecked, steel-blue flies poised in the air with vibrating wings. Their ears caught a gentle humming and buzzing all round them, and far away in the wood were heard now and again the tap-tap of the woodpecker and the screech of other birds.

"Listen," said Elisabeth, "I hear a bell."

"Where?" asked Reinhard.

"Behind us. Do you hear it? It is striking twelve o'clock."

"Then the town lies behind us, and if we go straight through in this direction we are bound to fall in with the others."

So they started on their homeward way; they had given up looking for strawberries, for Elisabeth had become tired. And at last there rang out from among the trees the laughing voices of the picnic party; then they saw too a white cloth spread gleaming on the ground; it was the luncheon-table and on it were strawberries enough and to spare.

The old gentleman had a table-napkin tucked in his button-hole and was continuing his moral sermon to the young folks and vigorously carving a joint of roast meat.

"Here come the stragglers," cried the young people when they saw Reinhard and Elisabeth advancing among the trees.

"This way," shouted the old gentleman. "Empty your handkerchiefs, upside down, with your hats! Now show us what you have found."

"Only hunger and thirst," said Reinhard.

"If that's all," replied the old man, lifting up and showing them the bowl full of fruit, "you must keep what you've got. You remember the agreement: nothing here for lazy-bones to eat."

But in the end he was prevailed on to relent; the banquet proceeded, and a thrush in a juniper bush provided the music.

So the day passed. But Reinhard had, after all, found something, and though it was not strawberries yet it was something that had grown in the wood. When he got home this is what he wrote in his old parchment-bound volume:

Out on the hill-side yonder
The wind to rest is laid;
Under the drooping branches
There sits the little maid.

She sits among the wild thyme,
She sits in the fragrant air;
The blue flies hum around her,
Bright wings flash everywhere.

And through the silent woodland
She peers with watchful eyen,
While on her hazel ringlets
Sparkles the glad sunshine.

And far, far off the cuckoo
Laughs out his song. I ween
Hers are the bright, the golden
Eyes of the woodland queen.

So she was not only his little sweetheart, but was also the expression of all that was lovely and wonderful in his opening life.

By the Roadside the Child Stood

The time is Christmas Eve. Before the close of the afternoon Reinhard and some other students were sitting together at an old oak table in the Ratskeller.*

The lamps on the wall were lighted, for down here in the basement it was already growing dark; but there was only a thin sprinkling of customers present, and the waiters were leaning idly up against the pillars let into the walls.

In a corner of the vaulted room sat a fiddler and a fine-featured gipsy-girl with a zither; their instruments lay in their laps, and they seemed to be looking about them with an air of indifference.

A champagne cork popped off at the table occupied by the students. "Drink, my gipsy darling!" cried a young man of aristocratic appearance, holding out to the girl a glass full of wine.

"I don't care about it," she said, without altering her position.

"Well, then, give us a song," cried the young nobleman, and threw a silver coin into her lap. The girl slowly ran her fingers through her black hair while the fiddler whispered in her ear. But she threw back her head, and rested her chin on her zither.

"For him," she said, "I'm not going to play."

Reinhard leapt up with his glass in his hand and stood in front of her.

"What do you want?" she asked defiantly.

"To have a look at your eyes."

"What have my eyes to do with you?"

Reinhard's glance flashed down on her. "I *know* they are false."

She laid her cheek in the palm of her hand and gave him a searching look. Reinhard raised his glass to his mouth.

"Here's to your beautiful, wicked eyes!" he said, and drank.

She laughed and tossed her head.

"Give it here," she said, and fastening her black eyes on his, she slowly drank what was left in the glass. Then she struck a chord and sang in a deep, passionate voice:

> To-day, to-day thou think'st me
> Fairest maid of all;
> To-morrow, ah! then beauty
> Fadeth past recall.

> While the hour remaineth,
> Thou art yet mine own;
> Then when death shall claim me,
> I must die alone.

While the fiddler struck up an allegro finale, a new arrival joined the group.

"I went to call for you, Reinhard," he said, "You had already gone out, but Santa Claus had paid you a visit."

"Santa Claus?" said Reinhard. "Santa Claus never comes to me now."

"Oh, yes, he does! The whole of your room smelt of Christmas tree and ginger cakes."

Reinhard dropped the glass out of his hand and seized his cap.

"Well, what are you going to do now?" asked the girl.

"I'll be back in a minute."

She frowned. "Stay," she said gently, casting an amorous glance at him.

Reinhard hesitated. "I can't," he said.

She laughingly gave him a tap with the toe of her shoe and said: "Go away, then, you good-for-nothing; you are one as bad as the other, all good-for-nothings." And as she turned away from him, Reinhard went slowly up the steps of the Ratskeller.

Outside in the street deep twilight had set in; he felt the cool winter air blowing on his heated brow. From some window every here and there fell the bright gleam of a Christmas tree all lighted up, now and then was heard from within some room the sound of little pipes and tin trumpets mingled with the merry din of children's voices.

Crowds of beggar children were going from house to house or climbing up on to the railings of the front steps, trying to catch a glimpse through the window of a splendour that was denied to them. Sometimes too a door would suddenly be flung open, and scolding voices would drive a whole swarm of these little visitors away out into the dark street. In the vestibule of yet another house they were singing an old Christmas carol, and little girls' clear voices were heard among the rest.

But Reinhard heard not; he passed quickly by them all, out of one street into another. When he reached his lodging it had grown almost quite dark; he stumbled up the stairs and so gained his apartment.

A sweet fragrance greeted him; it reminded him of home; it was the smell of the parlour in his mother's house at Christmas time. With trembling hand he lit his lamp; and there lay a mighty parcel on the table. When he opened it, out fell the familiar ginger cakes. On some of them were the initial letters of his name written in sprinkles of sugar; no one but Elisabeth could have done that.

Next came to view a little parcel containing neatly embroidered linen, handkerchiefs and cuffs; and finally letters from his mother and Elisabeth. Reinhard opened Elisabeth's letter first, and this is what she wrote:

"The pretty sugared letters will no doubt tell you who helped with the cakes. The same person also embroidered the cuffs for you. We shall have a very quiet time at home this Christmas Eve. Mother always puts her spinning-wheel away in the corner as early as half-past nine. It is so very lonesome this winter now that you are not here.

"And now, too, the linnet you made me a present of died last Sunday. It made me cry a good deal, though I am sure I looked after it well.

"It always used to sing of an afternoon when the sun shone on its cage. You remember how often mother would hang a piece of cloth over the cage in order to keep it quiet when it sang so lustily.

"Thus our room is now quieter than ever, except that your old friend Eric now drops in to see us occasionally. You told us once that he was just like his brown top-coat. I can't help thinking of it every time he comes in at the door, and it is really too funny; but don't tell mother, it might easily make her angry.

"Guess what I am giving your mother for a Christmas present! You can't guess? Well, it is myself! Eric is making a drawing of me in black chalk; I have had to give him three sittings, each time for a whole hour.

"I simply loathed the idea of a stranger getting to know my face so well. Nor did I wish it, but mother pressed me, and said it would very much please dear Frau Werner.

"But you are not keeping your word, Reinhard. You haven't sent me any stories. I have often complained to your mother about it, but she always says you now have more to do than to attend to such childish things. But I don't believe it; there's something else perhaps."

After this Reinhard read his mother's letter, and when he had read them both and slowly folded them up again and put them away, he was overcome with an irresistible feeling of home-sickness. For a long while he walked up and down his room, talking softly to himself, and then, under his breath, he murmured:

> I have err'd from the straight path,
> Bewildered I roam;
> By the roadside the child stands
> And beckons me home.

Then he went to his desk, took out some money, and stepped down into the street again. During all this while it had become quieter out there; the lights on the Christmas trees had burnt out, the processions of children had come to an end. The wind was sweeping through the deserted streets; old and young alike were sitting together at home in family parties; the second period of Christmas Eve celebrations had begun.

As Reinhard drew near the Ratskeller he heard from below the scraping of the fiddle and the singing of the zither girl. The restaurant door bell tinkled and a dark form staggered up the broad dimly-lighted stair.

Reinhard drew aside into the shadow of the houses and then passed swiftly by. After a while he reached the well-lighted shop of a jeweller, and after buying a little cross studded with red corals, he returned by the same way he had come.

Not far from his lodgings he caught sight of a little girl, dressed in miserable rags, standing before a tall door, in a vain attempt to open it.

"Shall I help you?" he said.

The child gave no answer, but let go the massive door-handle. Reinhard had soon opened the door.

"No," he said; "they might drive you out again. Come along with me, and I'll give you some Christmas cake."

He then closed the door again and gave his hand to the little girl, who walked along with him in silence to his lodgings.

On going out he had left the light burning.

"Here are some cakes for you," he said, pouring half of his whole stock into her apron, though he gave none that bore the sugar letters.

"Now, off you go home, and give your mother some of them too."

The child cast a shy look up at him; she seemed unaccustomed to such kindness and unable to say anything in reply. Reinhard opened the door, and lighted her way, and then the little thing like a bird flew downstairs with her cakes and out of the house.

Reinhard poked the fire in the stove, set the dusty inkstand on the table, and then sat down and wrote and wrote letters the whole night long to his mother and Elisabeth.

The remainder of the Christmas cakes lay untouched by his side, but he had buttoned on Elisabeth's cuffs, and odd they looked on his shaggy coat of undyed wool. And there he was still sitting when the winter sun cast its light on the frosted window-panes, and showed him a pale, grave face reflected in the looking-glass.

Home

When the Easter vacation came Reinhard journeyed home. On the morning after his arrival he went to see Elisabeth.

"How tall you've grown," he said, as the pretty, slender girl advanced with a smile to meet him. She blushed, but made no reply; he had taken her hand in his own in greeting, and she tried to draw it gently away. He looked at her doubtingly, for never had she done that before; but now it was as if some strange thing was coming between them.

The same feeling remained, too, after he had been at home for some time and came to see her constantly day after day. When they sat alone together there ensued pauses in the conversation which distressed him, and which he anxiously did his best to avoid. In order to have a definite occupation during the holidays, he began to give Elisabeth some instruction in botany, in which he himself had been keenly interested during the early months of his university career.

Elisabeth, who was wont to follow him in all things and was moreover very quick to learn, willingly entered into the proposal. So now several times in the week they made excursions into the fields or the moors, and if by midday they brought home their green field-box full of plants and flowers, Reinhard would come again later in the day and share with Elisabeth what they had collected in common.

With this same object in view, he entered the room one afternoon while Elisabeth was standing by the window and sticking some fresh chick-weed in a gilded birdcage which he had not seen in the place before. In the cage was a canary, which was flapping its wings and shrilly chirruping as it pecked at Elisabeth's fingers. Previously to this Reinhard's bird had hung in that spot.

"Has my poor linnet changed into a goldfinch after its death?" he asked jovially.

"Linnets are not accustomed to do any such thing," said Elizabeth's mother, who sat spinning in her armchair. "Your friend Eric sent it this noon from his estate as a present for Elisabeth."

"What estate?"

"Why, don't you know?"

"Know what?"

"That a month ago Eric took over his father's second estate by the Immensee." *

"But you have never said a word to me about it."

"Well," said the mother, "you haven't yet made a single word of inquiry after your friend. He is a very nice, sensible young man."

The mother went out of the room to make the coffee. Elisabeth had her back turned to Reinhard, and was still busy with the making of her little chickweed bower.

"Please, just a little longer," she said, "I'll be done in a minute."

As Reinhard did not answer, contrary to his wont, she turned round and faced him. In his eyes there was a sudden expression of trouble which she had never observed before in them.

"What is the matter with you, Reinhard?" she said, drawing nearer to him.

"With me?" he said, his thoughts far away and his eyes resting dreamily on hers.

"You look so sad."

"Elisabeth," he said, "I cannot bear that yellow bird."

She looked at him in astonishment, without understanding his meaning. "You are so strange," she said.

He took both her hands in his, and she let him keep them there. Her mother came back into the room shortly after; and after they had drunk their coffee she sat down at her spinning-wheel, while Reinhard and Elisabeth went off into the next room to arrange their plants.

Stamens were counted, leaves and blossoms carefully opened out, and two specimens of each sort were laid to dry between the pages of a large folio volume.

All was calm and still this sunny afternoon; the only sounds to be heard were the hum of the mother's spinning-wheel in the next room, and now and then the subdued voice of Reinhard, as he named the orders of the families of the plants, and corrected Elisabeth's awkward pronunciation of the Latin names.

"I am still short of that lily of the valley which I didn't get last time," said she, after the whole collection had been classified and arranged.

Reinhard pulled a little white vellum volume from his pocket. "Here is a spray of the lily of the valley for you," he said, taking out a half-pressed bloom.

When Elisabeth saw the pages all covered with writing, she asked: "Have you been writing stories again?"

"These aren't stories," he answered, handing her the book.

The contents were all poems, and the majority of them at most filled one page. Elisabeth turned over the leaves one after another; she appeared to be reading the titles only. "When she was scolded by the teacher." "When they lost their way in the woods." "An Easter story." "On her writing to me for the first time." Thus ran most of the titles.

Reinhard fixed his eyes on her with a searching look, and as she kept turning over the leaves he saw that a gentle blush arose and gradually mantled over the whole of her sweet face. He would fain have looked into her eyes, but Elisabeth did not look up, and finally laid the book down before him without a word.

"Don't give it back like that," he said.

She took a brown spray out of the tin case. "I will put your favourite flower inside," she said, giving back the book into his hands.

At length came the last day of the vacation and the morning of his departure. At her own request Elisabeth received permission from her mother to accompany her friend to the stage-coach, which had its station a few streets from their house.

When they passed out of the front door Reinhard gave her his arm, and thus he walked in silence side by side with the slender maiden. The nearer they came to their destination the more he felt as if he had something he must say to her before he bade her a long farewell, something on which all that was worthy and all that was sweet in his future life depended, and yet he could not formulate the saving word. In his anguish, he walked slower and slower.

"You'll be too late," she said; "it has already struck ten by St Mary's clock."

But he did not quicken his pace for all that. At last he stammered out:

"Elisabeth, you will not see me again for two whole years. Shall I be as dear to you as ever when I come back?"

She nodded, and looked affectionately into his face.

"I stood up for you too," she said, after a pause.

"Me? And against whom had you to stand up for me?"

"Against my mother. We were talking about you a long time yesterday evening after you left. She thought you were not so nice now as you once were."

Reinhard held his peace for a moment: then he took her hand in his, and looking gravely into her childish eyes, he said:

"I am still just as nice as I ever was; I would have you firmly believe that. Do you believe it, Elisabeth?"

"Yes," she said.

He freed her hand and quickly walked with her through the last street. The nearer he felt the time of parting approach, the happier became the look on his face; he went almost too quickly for her.

"What is the matter with you, Reinhard?" she asked.

"I have a secret, a beautiful secret," said Reinhard, looking at her with a light in his eyes. "When I come back again in two years' time, then you shall know it."

Meanwhile they had reached the stage-coach; they were only just in time. Once more Reinhard took her hand. "Farewell!" he said, "farewell, Elisabeth! Do not forget!"

She shook her head. "Farewell," she said. Reinhard climbed up into the coach and the horses started. As the coach rumbled round the corner of the street he saw her dear form once more as she slowly wended her way home.

A Letter

Nearly two years later Reinhard was sitting by lamplight with his books and papers around him, expecting a friend with whom he used to study in common. Some one came upstairs. "Come in." It was the landlady. "A letter for you, Herr Werner," and she went away.

Reinhard had never written to Elisabeth since his visit home, and he had received no letter from her. Nor was this one from her; it was in his mother's handwriting.

Reinhard broke the seal and read, and ere long he came to this paragraph:

"At your time of life, my dear boy, nearly every year still brings its own peculiar experience; for youth is apt to turn everything to the best account. At home, too, things have changed very much, and all this will, I fear, cause you much pain at first, if my understanding of you is at all correct.

"Yesterday Eric was at last accepted by Elisabeth, after having twice proposed in vain during the last three months. She had never been able to make up her mind to it, but now in the end she has done so. To my mind she is still far too young. The wedding is to take place soon, and her mother means to go away with them."

Immensee

Again years have passed. One warm afternoon in spring a young man, whose sunburnt face was the picture of health, was walking along a shady road through the wood leading down to the valley below.

His grave dark eyes looked intently into the distance, as though he was expecting to find every moment some change in the monotony of the road, a change however which seemed reluctant to come about. At length he saw a cart slowly coming up from below.

"Hullo! my friend," shouted the traveller to the farmer, who was walking by the side of the cart, "is this the right road to Immensee?"

"Yes, straight on," answered the man touching his slouch hat.

"Is it still far off?"

"You are close to the place, sir. In less time than it takes to smoke half a pipe of tobacco you'll be at the lake side, and the manor is hard by."

The farmer passed on while the other quickened his pace as he went along under the trees. After a quarter of an hour's walk the shade to the left of him suddenly came to an end; the road led along a steep slope from which the ancient oaks growing below hardly reared their topmost branches.

Away over their crests opened out a broad, sunny landscape. Far below lay the peaceful, dark-blue lake, almost entirely surrounded by green sun-lit woods, save where on one spot they divided and afforded an extensive view until it closed in the distant blue mountains.

Straight opposite, in the middle of all this forest verdure, there lay a patch of white, like driven snow. This was an expanse of blossoming fruit-trees, and out of them, up on the high lake shore, rose the manor-house, shining white, with tiles of red. A stork flew up from the chimney, and circled slowly above the waters.

"Immensee!" exclaimed the traveller.

It almost seemed as if he had now reached the end of his journey, for he stood motionless, looking out over the tops of the trees at his feet, and gazing at the farther shore, where the reflection of the manor-house floated, rocking gently, on the bosom of the water. Then he suddenly started on his way again.

His road now led almost steeply down the mountainside, so that the trees that had once stood below him again gave him their shade, but at the same time cut off from him the view of the lake, which only now and then peeped out between the gaps in the branches.

Soon the way went gently upwards again, and to left and right the woods disappeared, yielding place to vine-clad hills stretching along the pathway; while on either side stood fruit-trees in blossom, filled with the hum of the bees as they busily pried into the blossoms. A tall man wearing a brown overcoat advanced to meet the traveller. When he had almost come up to him, he waved his cap and cried out in a loud voice:

"Welcome, welcome, brother Reinhard! Welcome to my Immensee estate!"

"God's greeting to you,* Eric, and thank you for your welcome," replied the other.

By this time they had come up close to one another, and clasped hands.

"And is it really you?" said Eric, when he at last got a near sight of the grave face of his old school-fellow.

"It is I right enough, Eric, and I recognize you too; only you almost look cheerier than you ever did before."

At these words a glad smile made Eric's plain features all the more cheerful.

"Yes, brother Reinhard," he said, as he once more held out his hand to him, "but since those days, you see, I have won the great prize; but you know that well enough."

Then he rubbed his hands and cried cheerily: "This *will* be a surprise! You are the last person she expects to see."

"A surprise?" asked Reinhard. "For whom, pray?"

"Why, for Elisabeth."

"Elisabeth! You haven't told her a word about my visit?"

"Not a word, brother Reinhard; she has no thought of you, nor her mother either. I invited you entirely on the quiet, in order that the pleasure might be all the greater. You know I always had little quiet schemes of my own."

Reinhard turned thoughtful; he seemed to breathe more heavily the nearer they approached the house.

On the left side of the road the vineyards came to an end, and gave place to an extensive kitchen-garden, which reached almost as far as the lake-shore. The stork had meanwhile come to earth and was striding solemnly between the vegetable beds.

"Hullo!" cried Eric, clapping his hands together, "if that long-legged Egyptian isn't stealing my short pea-sticks again!"

The bird slowly rose and flew on to the roof of a new building, which ran along the end of the kitchen-garden, and whose walls were covered with the branches of the peach and apricot trees that were trained over them.

"That's the distillery," said Eric. "I built it only two years ago. My late father had the farm buildings rebuilt; the dwelling-house was built as far back as my grandfather's time. So we go ever forward a little bit at a time."

Talking thus they came to a wide, open space, enclosed at the sides by farm-buildings, and in the rear by the manor-house, the two wings of which were connected by a high garden wall. Behind this wall ran dark hedges of yew trees, while here and there syringa trees trailed their blossoming branches over into the courtyard.

Men with faces scorched by the sun and heated with toil were walking over the open space and gave a greeting to the two friends, while Eric called out to one or another of them some order or question about their day's work.

By this time they had reached the house. They entered a high, cool vestibule, at the far end of which they turned to the left into a somewhat darker passage.

Here Eric opened a door and they passed into a spacious room that opened into a garden. The heavy mass of leafage that covered the opposite windows filled this room at either end with a green twilight, while between the windows two lofty wide-open folding-doors let in the full glow of spring sunshine, and afforded a view into a garden, laid out with circular flower-beds and steep hedgerows and divided by a straight, broad path, along which the eye roamed out on to the lake and away over the woods growing on the opposite shore.

As the two friends entered, a breath of wind bore in upon them a perfect stream of fragrance.

On a terrace in front of the door leading to the garden sat a girlish figure dressed in white. She rose and came to meet the two friends as they entered, but half-way she stood stock-still as if rooted to the spot and stared at the stranger. With a smile he held out his hand to her.

"Reinhard!" she cried. "Reinhard! Oh! is it you? It is such a long time since we have seen each other."

"Yes, a long time," he said, and not a word more could he utter; for on hearing her voice he felt a keen, physical pain at his heart, and as he looked up to her, there she stood before him, the same slight, graceful figure to whom he had said farewell years ago in the town where he was born.

Eric had stood back by the door, with joy beaming from his eyes.

"Now, then, Elisabeth," he said, "isn't he really the very last person in the world you would have expected to see?"

Elisabeth looked at him with the eyes of a sister. "You are so kind, Eric," she said.

He took her slender hand caressingly in his. "And now that we have him," he said, "we shall not be in a hurry to

let him go. He has been so long away abroad, we will try
to make him feel at home again. Just see how foreign-look-
ing he has become, and what a distinguished appearance he
has!"

Elisabeth shyly scanned Reinhard's face. "The time that we
have been separated is enough to account for that," she said.

At this moment in at the door came her mother, key-bas-
ket on arm.

"Herr Werner!" she cried, when she caught sight of Reinhard; "ah! you are as dearly welcome as you are unexpected."

And so the conversation went smoothly on with questions and answers. The ladies sat over their work, and while
Reinhard enjoyed the refreshment that had been prepared
for him, Eric had lighted his huge meerschaum pipe and sat
smoking and conversing by his side.

Next day Reinhard had to go out with him to see the
fields, the vineyards, the hop-garden, the distillery. It was
all well appointed; the people who were working on the land
or at the vats all had a healthy and contented look.

For dinner the family assembled in the room that opened
into the garden, and the day was spent more or less in company just according to the leisure of the host and hostess.
Only during the hours preceding the evening meal, as also during the early hours of the forenoon, did Reinhard stay
working in his own room.

For some years past, whenever he could come across
them, he had been collecting the rhymes and songs that form
part of the life of the people, and now set about arranging
his treasure, and wherever possible increasing it by means
of fresh records from the immediate neighbourhood.

Elisabeth was at all times gentle and kind. Eric's constant attentions she received with an almost humble gratitude, and Reinhard thought at whiles that the gay, cheerful
child of bygone days had given promise of a somewhat less
sedate womanhood.

Ever since the second day of his visit he had been wont
of an evening to take a walk along the shore of the lake. The
road led along close under the garden. At the end of the latter,

on a projecting mound, there was a bench under some tall birch trees. Elisabeth's mother had christened it the Evening Bench, because the spot faced westward, and was mostly used at that time of the day in order to enjoy a view of the sunset.

One evening Reinhard was returning from his walk along this road when he was overtaken by the rain. He sought shelter under one of the linden trees that grew by the water-side, but the heavy drops were soon pelting through the leaves. Wet through as he was he resigned himself to his fate and slowly continued his homeward way.

It was almost dark; the rain fell faster and faster. As he drew near to the Evening Bench he fancied he could make out the figure of a woman dressed in white standing among the gleaming birch tree trunks. She stood motionless, and, as far as he could make out on approaching nearer, with her face turned in his direction, as if she was expecting some one.

He thought it was Elisabeth. But when he quickened his pace in order that he might catch up to her and then return together with her through the garden into the house, she turned slowly away and disappeared among the dark side-paths.

He could not understand it; he was almost angry with Elisabeth, and yet he doubted whether it had really been she. He was, however, shy of questioning her about it—nay, he even avoided going into the garden-room on his return to the house for fear he should happen to see Elisabeth enter through the garden-door.

By my Mother's Hard Decree

Some days later, as evening was already closing in, the family was, as usual at this time of the day, sitting all together in their garden-room. The doors stood wide open, and the sun had already sunk behind the woods on the far side of the lake.

Reinhard was invited to read some folk-songs which had been sent to him that afternoon by a friend who lived away in the country. He went up to his room and soon returned with a roll of papers which seemed to consist of detached neatly written pages.

So they all sat down to the table, Elisabeth beside Reinhard. "We shall read them at random," said the latter, "I have not yet looked through them myself."

Elisabeth unrolled the manuscript. "Here's some music," she said, "you must sing it, Reinhard."

To begin with he read some Tyrolese ditties* and as he read on he would now and then hum one or other of the lively melodies. A general feeling of cheeriness pervaded the little party.

"And who, pray, made all these pretty songs?" asked Elisabeth.

"Oh," said Eric, "you can tell that by listening to the rubbishy things—tailors' apprentices and barbers and such-like merry folk."

Reinhard said: "They are not made; they grow, they drop from the clouds, they float over the land like gossamer,* hither and thither, and are sung in a thousand places at the same time. We discover in these songs our very inmost activities and sufferings: it is as if we all had helped to write them."

He took up another sheet: "I stood on the mountain height..." *

"I know that one," cried Elisabeth; "begin it, do, Reinhard, and I will help you out."

So they sang that famous melody, which is so mysterious that one can hardly believe that it was ever conceived by the heart of man, Elisabeth with her slightly clouded contralta taking the second part to the young man's tenor.

The mother meanwhile sat busy with her needlework, while Eric listened attentively, with one hand clasped in the other. The song finished, Reinhard laid the sheet on one side in silence. Up from the lake-shore came through the evening calm the tinkle of the cattle bells; they were all listening without knowing why, and presently they heard a boy's clear voice singing:

I stood on the mountain height
And viewed the deep valley beneath....

Reinhard smiled. "Do you hear that now? So it passes from mouth to mouth."

"It is often sung in these parts," said Elisabeth.

"Yes," said Eric, "it is Casper the herdsman; he is driving the heifers* home."

They listened a while longer until the tinkle of the bells died away behind the farm buildings. "These melodies are as old as the world," said Reinhard; "they slumber in the depths of the forest; God knows who discovered them."

He drew forth a fresh sheet.

It had now grown darker; a crimson evening glow lay like foam over the woods in the farther side of the lake. Reinhard unrolled the sheet, Elisabeth caught one side of it in her hand, and they both examined it together. Then Reinhard read:

By my mother's hard decree Another's wife I needs must be; Him on whom my heart was set, Him, alas! I must forget; My heart protesting, but not free.

Bitterly did I complain That my mother brought me pain. What mine honour might have been, That is turned to deadly sin. Can I ever hope again?

For my pride what can I show, And my joy, save grief and woe? h! could I undo what's done, O'er the moor scorched by the sun Beggarwise I'd gladly go.

During the reading of this Reinhard had felt an imperceptible quivering of the paper; and when he came to an end Elisabeth gently pushed her chair back and passed silently out into the garden. Her mother followed her with a look. Eric made as if to go after, but the mother said:

"Elisabeth has one or two little things to do outside," so he remained where he was.

But out of doors the evening brooded darker and darker over garden and lake. Moths whirred past the open doors through which the fragrance of flower and bush floated in increasingly; up from the water came the croak of the frogs, under the windows a nightingale commenced his song answered by another from within the depths of the garden; the moon appeared over the tree-tops.

Reinhard looked for a little while longer at the spot where Elisabeth's sweet form had been lost to sight in the thick-foliaged garden paths, and then he rolled up his manuscript, bade his friends good-night and passed through the house down to the water.

The woods stood silent and cast their dark shadow far out over the lake, while the centre was bathed in the haze of a pale moonlight. Now and then a gentle rustle trembled through the trees, though wind there was none; it was but the breath of summer night.

Reinhard continued along the shore. A stone's throw from the land he perceived a white water-lily. All at once he was seized with the desire to see it quite close, so he threw off his clothes and entered the water. It was quite shallow; sharp stones and water plants cut his feet, and yet he could not reach water deep enough for him to swim in.

Then suddenly he stepped out of his depth: the waters swirled above him; and it was some time before he rose to the surface again. He struck out with hands and feet and swam about in a circle until he had made quite sure from what point he had entered the water. And soon too he saw the lily again floating lonely among the large, gleaming leaves.

He swam slowly out, lifting every now and then his arms out of the water so that the drops trickled down and sparkled in the moonlight. Yet the distance between him and the flower showed no signs of diminishing, while the shore, as he glanced back at it, showed behind him in a hazy mist that ever deepened. But he refused to give up the venture and vigorously continued swimming in the same direction.

At length he had come so near the flower that he was able clearly to distinguish the silvery leaves in the moonlight; but at the same time he felt himself entangled in a net formed by the smooth stems of the water plants which swayed up from the bottom and wound themselves round his naked limbs.

The unfamiliar water was black all round about him, and behind him he heard the sound of a fish leaping. Suddenly such an uncanny feeling overpowered him in the midst of this strange element that with might and main he tore asunder the network of plants and swam back to land in breathless haste. And when from the shore he looked back upon the lake, there floated the lily on the bosom of the darkling water as far away and as lonely as before.

He dressed and slowly wended his way home. As he passed out of the garden into the room he discovered Eric and the mother busied with preparations for a short journey which had to be undertaken for business purposes on the morrow.

"Where ever have you been so late in the dark?" the mother called out to him.

"I?" he answered, "oh, I wanted to pay a call on the water-lily, but I failed."

"That's beyond the comprehension of any man," said Eric. "What on earth had you to do with the water-lily?"

"Oh, I used to be friends with the lily once," said Reinhard; "but that was long ago."

Elisabeth

The following afternoon Reinhard and Elisabeth went for a walk on the farther side of the lake, strolling at times through the woodland, at other times along the shore where it jutted out into the water. Elisabeth had received injunctions from Eric, during the absence of himself and her mother to show Reinhard the prettiest views in the immediate neighbourhood, particularly the view toward the farm itself from the other side of the lake. So now they proceeded from one point to another.

At last Elisabeth got tired and sat down in the shade of some overhanging branches. Reinhard stood opposite to her, leaning against a tree trunk; and as he heard the cuckoo calling farther back in the woods, it suddenly struck him that all this had happened once before. He looked at her and with an odd smile asked:

"Shall we look for strawberries?"

"It isn't strawberry time," she said.

"No, but it will soon be here."

Elisabeth shook her head in silence; then she rose and the two strolled on together. And as they wandered side by side, his eyes ever and again were bent toward her; for she walked gracefully and her step was light. He often unconsciously fell back a pace in order that he might feast his eyes on a full view of her.

So they came to an open space overgrown with heather where the view extended far over the country-side. Reinhard bent down and plucked a bloom from one of the little plants that grew at his feet. When he looked up again there was an expression of deep pain on his face.

"Do you know this flower?" he asked.

She gave him a questioning look. "It is an erica. I have often gathered them in the woods."

"I have an old book at home," he said; "I once used to write in it all sorts of songs and rhymes, but that is all over and done with long since. Between its leaves also there is an erica, but it is only a faded one. Do you know who gave it me?"

She nodded without saying a word; but she cast down her eyes and fixed them on the bloom which he held in his hand. For a long time they stood thus. When she raised her eyes on him again he saw that they were brimming over with tears.

"Elisabeth," he said, "behind yonder blue hills lies our youth. What has become of it?"

Nothing more was spoken. They walked dumbly by each other's side down to the lake. The air was sultry; to westward dark clouds were rising. "There's going to be a storm," said Elisabeth, hastening her steps. Reinhard nodded in silence, and together they rapidly sped along the shore till they reached their boat.

On the way across Elisabeth rested her hand on the gunwale of the boat. As he rowed Reinhard glanced along at her, but she gazed past him into the distance. And so his glance fell downward and rested on her hand, and the white hand betrayed to him what her lips had failed to reveal.

It revealed those fine traces of secret pain that so readily mark a woman's fair hands, when they lie at nights folded across an aching heart. And as Elisabeth felt his glance resting on her hand she let it slip gently over the gunwale into the water.

On arriving at the farm they fell in with a scissors grinder's cart standing in front of the manor-house. A man with black, loosely-flowing hair was busily plying his wheel and humming a gipsy melody between his teeth, while a dog that was harnessed to the cart lay panting hard by. On the threshold stood a girl dressed in rags, with features of faded beauty, and with outstretched hand she asked alms of Elisabeth.

Reinhard thrust his hand into his pocket, but Elisabeth was before him, and hastily emptied the entire contents of her purse into the beggar's open palm. Then she turned quickly away, and Reinhard heard her go sobbing up the stairs.

He would fain have detained her, but he changed his mind and remained at the foot of the stairs. The beggar girl was still standing at the doorway, motionless, and holding in her hand the money she had received.

"What more do you want?" asked Reinhard.

She gave a sudden start: "I want nothing more," she said; then, turning her head toward him and staring at him with wild eyes, she passed slowly out of the door. He uttered a name, but she heard him not; with drooping head, with arms folded over her breast, she walked down across the farmyard:

> Then when death shall claim me,
> I must die alone.

An old song surged in Reinhard's ears, he gasped for breath; a little while only, and then he turned away and went up to his chamber.

He sat down to work, but his thoughts were far afield. After an hour's vain attempt he descended to the parlour. Nobody was in it, only cool, green twilight; on Elisabeth's work-table lay a red ribbon which she had worn round her neck during the afternoon. He took it up in his hand, but it hurt him, and he laid it down again.

He could find no rest. He walked down to the lake and untied the boat. He rowed over the water and trod once again all the paths which he and Elisabeth had paced together but a short hour ago. When he got back home it was dark. At the farm he met the coachman, who was about to turn the carriage horses out into the pasture; the travellers had just returned.

As he came into the entrance hall he heard Eric pacing up and down the garden-room. He did not go in to him; he stood still for a moment, and then softly climbed the stairs and so to his own room. Here he sat in the arm-chair by the window. He made himself believe that he was listening to the nightingale's throbbing music in the garden hedges below, but what he heard was the throbbing of his own heart. Downstairs in the house every one went to bed, the night-hours passed, but he paid no heed.

For hours he sat thus, till at last he rose and leaned out of the open window. The dew was dripping among the leaves, the nightingale had ceased to trill. By degrees the deep blue of the darksome sky was chased away by a faint yellow gleam that came from the east; a fresh wind rose and brushed Reinhard's heated brow; the early lark soared triumphant up into the sky.

Reinhard suddenly turned and stepped up to the table. He groped about for a pencil and when he had found one he sat down and wrote a few lines on a sheet of white paper. Having finished his writing he took up hat and stick, and leaving the paper behind him, carefully opened the door and descended to the vestibule.

The morning twilight yet brooded in every corner; the big house-cat stretched its limbs on the straw mat and arched its back against Reinhard's hand, which he unthinkingly held out to it. Outside in the garden the sparrows were already chirping their patter* from among the branches, and giving notice to all that the night was now past.

Then within the house he heard a door open on the upper floor; some one came downstairs, and on looking up he saw Elisabeth standing before him. She laid her hand upon his arm, her lips moved, but not a word did he hear.

Presently she said: "You will never come back. I know it; do not deny it; you will never come back."

"No, never," he said.

She let her hand fall from his arm and said no more. He crossed the hall to the door, then turned once more. She was standing motionless on the same spot and looking at him with lifeless eyes. He advanced one step and opened his arms toward her; then, with a violent effort, he turned away and so passed out of the door.

Outside the world lay bathed in morning light, the drops of pearly dew caught on the spiders' webs glistened in the first rays of the rising sun. He never looked back; he walked rapidly onward; behind him the peaceful farmstead gradually disappeared from view as out in front of him rose the great wide world.

The Old Man

The moon had ceased to shine in through the window-panes, and it had grown quite dark; but the old man still sat in his arm-chair with folded hands and gazed before him into the emptiness of the room.

Gradually. the murky darkness around him dissolved away before his eyes and changed into a broad dark lake; one black wave after another went rolling on farther and farther, and on the last one, so far away as to be almost beyond the reach of the old man's vision, floated lonely among its broad leaves a white water-lily.

The door opened, and a bright glare of light filled the room.

"I am glad that you have come, Bridget," said the old man. "Set the lamp upon the table."

Then he drew his chair up to the table, took one of the open books and buried himself in studies to which he had once applied all the strength of his youth.

Notes
(marked with *)

"There were once upon a time three spinning-women...": The beginning of one of the best known of Grimm's fairy tales.

Ratskeller: The basement of the Rathaus or Town Hall. This, in almost every German town of importance, has become a restaurant and place of refreshment.

Immensee: I.e. the 'Lake of the Bees'

God's greeting to you: This form of salutation is especially common in the south of Germany.

Tyrolese ditties: Dialectal for *Schnitterhüpfen* , i.e. 'reapers' dances,' sung especially in the Tyrol and in Bavaria.

Gossamer: These fine cobwebs, produced by field-spiders, have always in the popular mind been connected with the gods. After the advent of Christianity they were connected with the Virgin Mary. The shroud in which she was wrapped after her death was believed to have been woven of the very finest thread, which during her ascent to Heaven frayed away from her body.

"I stood on the mountain height...": An ancient folk-song which treats of a beautiful but poor maiden, who, being unable to marry 'the young count,' retired to a convent.

Heifers: Starke is the southern dialect word for *Färse* , 'young cow,' 'heifer.'

The sparrows were already chirping their patter: Literally, "sang out pompously, like priests." The word seems to have been coined by the author. The English 'patter' is derived from *Pater noster* , and seems an appropriate translation.

Adelbert von Chamisso

Peter Schlemihl
The Shadowless Man

Introductory Epistle from
Adelbert von Chamisso
to Julius Edward Hitzig

You, who forget nobody, must surely re-member one Peter Schlemihl, whom you used to meet occasionally at my house—a long-legged youth, who was considered stupid and lazy, on account of his awkward and careless air. I was sincerely attached to him. You cannot have forgotten him, Edward. He was on one occasion the hero of our rhymes, in the hey-day of our youthful spirits; and I recollect taking him one evening to a poetical tea-party, where he fell asleep while I was writing, without even waiting to hear my effusion: and this reminds me of a witticism of yours respecting him. You had already seen him, I know not where or when, in an old black frock-coat, which, indeed, he constantly wore; and you said, "He would be a lucky fellow if his soul were half as immortal as his coat," so little opinion had you of him. *I* loved him, however: and to this very Schlemihl, of whom for many years I had wholly lost sight, I am indebted for the little volume which I communicate to you, Edward, my most intimate friend, my second self, from whom I have no secrets;—to you, and of course our Fouqué, I commit them, who like you is intimately entwined about my dearest affections,—to him I communicate them only as a friend, but not as a poet; for you can easily imagine how unpleasant it would be if a secret confided to me by an honest man, relying implicitly on my friendship and honour, were to be exposed to the public in a poem.

One word more as to the manner in which I obtained these sheets: yesterday morning early, as soon as I was up, they were brought to me. An extraordinary-looking man, with a long grey beard, and wearing an old black frock-coat with a botanical case hanging at his side, and slippers over his boots, in the damp, rainy weather, had just been inquiring for me, and left me these papers, saying he came from Berlin.

Adelbert von Chamisso

Chapter I

After a prosperous, but to me very wearisome, voyage, we came at last into port. Immediately on landing I got together my few effects; and, squeezing myself through the crowd, went into the nearest and humblest inn which first met my gaze. On asking for a room the waiter looked at me from head to foot, and conducted me to one. I asked for some cold water, and for the correct address of Mr. Thomas John, which was described as being "by the north gate, the first country-house to the right, a large new house of red and white marble, with many pillars." This was enough. As the day was not yet far advanced, I untied my bundle, took out my newly-turned black coat, dressed myself in my best clothes, and, with my letter of recommendation, set out for the man who was to assist me in the attainment of my moderate wishes.

After proceeding up the north street, I reached the gate, and saw the marble columns glittering through the trees. Having wiped the dust from my shoes with my pocket-handkerchief and readjusted my cravat, I rang the bell— offering up at the same time a silent prayer. The door flew open, and the porter sent in my name. I had soon the honour to be invited into the park, where Mr. John was walking with a few friends. I recognised him at once by his corpulency and self-complacent air. He received me very well—

just as a rich man receives a poor devil; and turning to me, took my letter. "Oh, from my brother! it is a long time since I heard from him: is he well?—Yonder," he went on,—turning to the company, and pointing to a distant hill—"Yonder is the site of the new building." He broke the seal without discontinuing the conversation, which turned upon riches. "The man," he said, "who does not possess at least a million is a poor wretch." – "Oh, how true!" I exclaimed, in the fulness of my heart. He seemed pleased at this, and replied with a smile, "Stop here, my dear friend; afterwards I shall, perhaps, have time to tell you what I think of this," pointing to the letter, which he then put into his pocket, and turned round to the company, offering his arm to a young lady: his example was followed by the other gentlemen, each politely escorting a lady; and the whole party proceeded towards a little hill thickly planted with blooming roses.

I followed without troubling any one, for none took the least further notice of me. The party was in high spirits—lounging about and jesting—speaking sometimes of trifling matters very seriously, and of serious matters as triflingly—and exercising their wit in particular to great advantage on their absent friends and their affairs. I was too ignorant of what they were talking about to understand much of it, and too anxious and absorbed in my own reflections to occupy myself with the solution of such enigmas as their conversation presented.

By this time we had reached the thicket of roses. The lovely Fanny, who seemed to be the queen of the day, was obstinately bent on plucking a rose-branch for herself, and in the attempt pricked her finger with a thorn. The crimson stream, as if flowing from the dark-tinted rose, tinged her fair hand with the purple current. This circumstance set the whole company in commotion; and court-plaster was called for. A quiet, elderly man, tall, and meagre-looking, who was one of the company, but whom I had not before observed, immediately put his hand into the tight breast-pocket of his old-fashioned coat of grey sarsnet, pulled out a small letter-case, opened it, and, with a most respectful bow, presented the lady with the wished-for article. She received it without noticing the giver, or thanking him. The wound was bound up, and the party proceeded along the hill towards the back part, from which they enjoyed an extensive view across the green labyrinth of the park to the wide-spreading ocean. The view was truly a magnificent one. A slight speck was observed on the horizon, between the dark flood and the azure sky. "A telescope!" called out Mr. John; but before any of the servants could answer the summons the grey man, with a modest bow, drew his hand from his pocket, and presented a beautiful Dollond's telescope to Mr. John, who, on looking through it, informed the company that the speck in the distance was the ship which had sailed yesterday, and which was detained within sight of the haven by contrary winds. The telescope passed from hand to hand, but was not returned to the owner, whom I gazed at with astonishment, and could not conceive how so large an instrument could have proceeded from so small a pocket. This, however, seemed to excite surprise in no one; and the grey man appeared to create as little interest as myself.

Refreshments were now brought forward, consisting of the rarest fruits from all parts of the world, served up in the most costly dishes. Mr. John did the honours with unaffected grace, and addressed me for the second time, saying, "You had better eat; you did not get such things at sea." I acknowledged his politeness with a bow, which, however, he did not perceive, having turned round to speak with some one else.

The party would willingly have stopped some time here on the declivity of the hill, to enjoy the extensive prospect before them, had they not been apprehensive of the dampness of the grass. "How delightful it would be," exclaimed some one, "if we had a Turkey carpet to lay down here!" The wish was scarcely expressed when the man in the grey coat put his hand in his pocket, and, with a modest and even humble air, pulled out a rich Turkey carpet, embroidered in gold. The servant received it as a matter of course, and spread it out on the desired spot; and, without any ceremony, the company seated themselves on it. Confounded by what I saw, I gazed again at the man, his pocket, and the carpet, which was more than twenty feet in length and ten in breadth; and rubbed my eyes, not knowing what to think, particularly as no one saw anything extraordinary in the matter. I would gladly have made some inquiries respecting the man, and asked who he was, but knew not to whom I should address myself, for I felt almost more afraid of the servants than of their master. At length I took courage, and stepping up to a young man who seemed of less consequence than the others, and who was more frequently standing by himself, I begged of him, in a low tone, to tell me who the obliging gentleman was in the grey cloak. "That man who looks like a piece of thread just escaped from a tailor's needle?" "Yes; he who is standing alone yonder." – "I do not know," was the reply; and to avoid, as it seemed, any further conversation with me, he turned away, and spoke of some common-place matters with a neighbour.

The sun's rays now being stronger, the ladies complained of feeling oppressed by the heat; and the lovely Fanny, turning carelessly to the grey man, to whom I had not yet observed that any one had addressed the most trifling question, asked him if, perhaps, he had not a tent about him. He replied, with a low bow, as if some unmerited honour had been conferred upon him; and, putting his hand in his pocket, drew from it canvas, poles, cord, iron—in short, everything belonging to the most splendid tent for a party of pleasure. The young gentlemen assisted in pitching it: and it covered the whole carpet: but no one seemed to think that there was anything extraordinary in it.

I had long secretly felt uneasy—indeed, almost horrified; but how was this feeling increased when, at the next wish expressed, I saw him take from his pocket three horses! Yes, Adelbert, three large beautiful steeds, with saddles and bridles, out of the very pocket whence had already issued a letter-case, a telescope, a carpet twenty feet broad and ten in length, and a pavilion of the same extent, with all its appurtenances! Did I not assure thee that my own eyes had seen all this, thou wouldst certainly disbelieve it.

This man, although he appeared so humble and embarrassed in his air and manners, and passed so unheeded, had inspired me with such a feeling of horror by the unearthly paleness of his countenance, from which I could not avert my eyes, that I was unable longer to endure it.

I determined, therefore, to steal away from the company, which appeared no difficult matter, from the undistinguished part I acted in it. I resolved to return to the town, and pay another visit to Mr. John the following morning, and, at the same time, make some inquiries of him relative to the extraordinary man in grey, provided I could command sufficient courage. Would to Heaven that such good fortune had awaited me!

I had stolen safely down the hill, through the thicket of roses, and now found myself on an open plain; but fearing lest I should be met out of the proper path, crossing the grass, I cast an inquisitive glance around, and started as I beheld the man in the grey cloak advancing towards me. He took off his hat, and made me a lower bow than mortal had ever yet favoured me with. It was evident that he wished to address me; and I could not avoid encountering him without seeming rude. I returned his salutation, therefore, and stood bareheaded in the sunshine as if rooted to the ground. I gazed at him with the utmost horror, and felt like a bird fascinated by a serpent.

He affected himself to have an air of embarrassment. With his eyes on the ground, he bowed several times, drew nearer, and at last, without looking up, addressed me in a low and hesitating voice, almost in the tone of a suppliant: "Will you, sir, excuse my importunity in venturing to intrude upon you in so unusual a manner? I have a request to make—would you most graciously be pleased to allow me—!" – "Hold! for Heaven's sake!" I exclaimed; "what can I do for a man who"—I stopped in some confusion, which he seemed to share. After a moment's pause, he resumed: "During the short time I have had the pleasure to be in your company, I have—permit me, sir, to say—beheld with unspeakable admiration your most beautiful shadow, and remarked the air of noble indifference with which you, at the same time, turn from the glorious picture at your feet, as if disdaining to vouchsafe a glance at it. Excuse the boldness of my proposal; but perhaps you would have no objection to sell me your shadow?" He stopped, while my head turned round like a mill-wheel. What was I to think of so extraordinary a proposal? To sell my shadow! "He must be mad," thought I; and assuming a tone more in character with the submissiveness of his own, I replied, "My good friend, are you not content with your own shadow? This would be a bargain of a strange nature indeed!"

"I have in my pocket," he said, "many things which may possess some value in your eyes: for that inestimable shadow I should deem the highest price too little."

A cold shuddering came over me as I recollected the pocket; and I could not conceive what had induced me to style him *"Good Friend,"* which I took care not to repeat, endeavouring to make up for it by a studied politeness.

I now resumed the conversation: —"But, Sir—excuse your humble servant—I am at a loss to comprehend your meaning,—my shadow?—how can I?"

"Permit me," he exclaimed, interrupting me, "to gather up the noble image as it lies on the ground, and to take it into my possession. As to the manner of accomplishing it, leave that to me. In return, and as an evidence of my gratitude, I shall leave you to choose among all the treasures I have in my pocket, among which are a variety of enchanting articles, not exactly adapted for you, who, I am sure, would like better to have the wishing-cap of Fortunatus, all made new and sound again, and a lucky purse which also belonged to him."

"Fortunatus's purse!" cried I; and, great as was my mental anguish, with that one word he had penetrated the deepest recesses of my soul. A feeling of giddiness came over me, and double ducats glittered before my eyes.

"Be pleased, gracious sir, to examine this purse, and make a trial of its contents." He put his hand in his pocket, and drew forth a large strongly stitched bag of stout Cordovan leather, with a couple of strings to match, and presented it to me. I seized it—took out ten gold pieces, then ten more, and this I repeated again and again. Instantly I held out my hand to him. "Done," said I; "the bargain is made: my shadow for the purse." "Agreed," he answered; and, immediately kneeling down, I beheld him, with extraordinary dexterity, gently loosen my shadow from the grass, lift it up, fold it together, and, at last put it in his pocket. He then rose, bowed once more to me, and directed his steps towards the rose bushes. I fancied I heard him quietly laughing to himself. However, I held the purse fast by the two strings. The earth was basking beneath the brightness of the sun; but I presently lost all consciousness.

On recovering my senses, I hastened to quit a place where I hoped there was nothing further to detain me. I first filled my pockets with gold, then fastened the strings of the purse round my neck, and concealed it in my bosom. I passed unnoticed out of the park, gained the high road, and took the way to the town. As I was thoughtfully approaching the gate, I heard some one behind me exclaiming, "Young man! young man! you have lost your shadow!" I turned, and perceived an old woman calling after me. "Thank you, my good woman," said I; and throwing her a piece of gold for her well-intended information, I stepped under the trees. At the gate, again, it was my fate to hear the sentry inquiring where the gentleman had left his shadow; and immediately I heard a couple of women exclaiming, "Jesu Maria! the poor man has no shadow." All this began to depress me, and I carefully avoided walking in the sun; but this could not everywhere be the case: for in the next broad street I had to cross, and, unfortunately for me, at the very hour in which the boys were coming out of school, a humpbacked lout of a fellow—I see him yet—soon made the discovery that I was without a shadow, and communicated the news, with loud outcries, to a knot of young urchins. The whole swarm proceeded immediately to reconnoitre me, and to pelt me with mud. "People," cried they, "are generally accustomed to take their shadows with them when they walk in the sunshine."

In order to drive them away I threw gold by handfuls among them, and sprang into a hackney-coach which some compassionate spectators sent to my rescue.

As soon as I found myself alone in the rolling vehicle I began to weep bitterly. I had by this time a misgiving that, in the same degree in which gold in this world prevails over merit and virtue, by so much one's shadow excels gold; and now that I had sacrificed my conscience for riches, and given my shadow in exchange for mere gold, what on earth would become of me?

As the coach stopped at the door of my late inn, I felt much perplexed, and not at all disposed to enter so wretched an abode. I called for my things, and received them with an air of contempt, threw down a few gold pieces, and desired to be conducted to a first-rate hotel. This house had a northern aspect, so that I had nothing to fear from the sun. I dismissed the coachman with gold; asked to be conducted to the best apartment, and locked myself up in it as soon as possible.

Imagine, my friend, what I then set about? O my dear Chamisso! even to thee I blush to mention what follows.

I drew the ill-fated purse from my bosom; and, in a sort of frenzy that raged like a self-fed fire within me, I took out gold—gold—gold—more and more, till I strewed it on the floor, trampled upon it, and feasting on its very sound and brilliancy, added coins to coins, rolling and revelling on the gorgeous bed, until I sank exhausted.

Thus passed away that day and evening; and as my door remained locked, night found me still lying on the gold, where, at last, sleep overpowered me.

Then I dreamed of thee, and fancied I stood behind the glass door of thy little room, and saw thee seated at thy table between a skeleton and a bunch of dried plants; before thee lay open the works of Haller, Humboldt, and Linnaeus; on thy sofa a volume of Goethe, and the Enchanted Ring. I stood a long time contemplating thee, and everything in thy apartment; and again turning my gaze upon thee, I perceived that thou wast motionless—thou didst not breathe—thou wast dead.

I awoke—it seemed yet early—my watch had stopped. I felt thirsty, faint, and worn out; for since the preceding morning I had not tasted food. I now cast from me, with loathing and disgust, the very gold with which but a short time before I had satiated my foolish heart. Now I knew not where to put it—I dared not leave it lying there. I examined my purse to see if it would hold it,—impossible! Neither of my windows opened on the sea. I had no other resource but, with toil and great fatigue, to drag it to a huge chest which stood in a closet in my room; where I placed it all, with the exception of a handful or two. Then I threw myself, exhausted, into an arm-chair, till the people of the house should be up and stirring. As soon as possible I sent for some refreshment, and desired to see the landlord.

I entered into some conversation with this man respecting the arrangement of my future establishment. He recommended for my personal attendant one Bendel, whose honest and intelligent countenance immediately pre-possessed me in his favour. It is this individual whose persevering attachment has consoled me in all the miseries of my life, and enabled me to bear up under my wretched lot. I was occupied the whole day in my room with servants in want of a situation, and tradesmen of every description. I decided on my future plans, and purchased various articles of vertu and splendid jewels, in order to get rid of some of my gold; but nothing seemed to diminish the inexhaustible heap.

I now reflected on my situation with the utmost uneasiness. I dared not take a single step beyond my own door; and in the evening I had forty wax tapers lighted before I ventured to leave the shade. I reflected with horror on the frightful encounter with the school-boys; yet I resolved, if I could command sufficient courage, to put the public opinion to a second trial. The nights were now moon-light. Late in the evening I wrapped myself in a large cloak, pulled my hat over my eyes, and, trembling like a criminal, stole out of the house.

I did not venture to leave the friendly shadow of the houses until I had reached a distant part of the town; and then I emerged into the broad moonlight, fully prepared to hear my fate from the lips of the passers-by.

Spare me, my beloved friend, the painful recital of all that I was doomed to endure. The women often expressed the deepest sympathy for me—a sympathy not less piercing to my soul than the scoffs of the young people, and the proud contempt of the men, particularly of the more corpulent, who threw an ample shadow before them. A fair and beauteous maiden, apparently accompanied by her parents, who gravely kept looking straight before them, chanced to cast a beaming glance on me; but was evidently startled at perceiving that I was without a shadow, and hiding her lovely face in her veil, and holding down her head, passed silently on.

This was past all endurance. Tears streamed from my eyes; and with a heart pierced through and through, I once more took refuge in the shade. I leant on the houses for support, and reached home at a late hour, worn out with fatigue.

I passed a sleepless night. My first care the following morning was, to devise some means of discovering the man in the grey cloak. Perhaps I may succeed in finding him; and how fortunate it were if he should be as ill satisfied with his bargain as I am with mine!

I desired Bendel to be sent for, who seemed to possess some tact and ability. I minutely described to him the individual who possessed a treasure without which life itself was rendered a burden to me. I mentioned the time and place at which I had seen him, named all the persons who were present, and concluded with the following directions: —He was to inquire for a Dollond's telescope, a Turkey carpet interwoven with gold, a marquee, and, finally, for some black steeds—the history, without entering into particulars, of all these being singularly connected with the mysterious character who seemed to pass unnoticed by every one, but whose appearance had destroyed the peace and happiness of my life.

As I spoke I produced as much gold as I could hold in my two hands, and added jewels and precious stones of still greater value. "Bendel," said I, "this smooths many a path, and renders that easy which seems almost impossible. Be not sparing of it, for I am not so; but go, and rejoice thy master with intelligence on which depend all his hopes."

He departed, and returned late and melancholy.

None of Mr. John's servants, none of his guests (and Bendel had spoken to them all) had the slightest recollection of the man in the grey cloak.

The new telescope was still there, but no one knew how it had come; and the tent and Turkey carpet were still stretched out on the hill. The servants boasted of their master's wealth; but no one seemed to know by what means he had become possessed of these newly acquired luxuries. He was gratified; and it gave him no concern to be ignorant how they had come to him. The black coursers which had been mounted on that day were in the stables of the young gentlemen of the party, who admired them as the munificent present of Mr. John.

Such was the information I gained from Bendel's detailed account; but, in spite of this unsatisfactory result, his zeal and prudence deserved and received my commendation. In a gloomy mood, I made him a sign to with-draw.

"I have, sir," he continued, "laid before you all the information in my power relative to the subject of the most importance to you. I have now a message to deliver which I received early this morning from a person at the gate, as I was proceeding to execute the commission in which I have so unfortunately failed. The man's words were precisely these: ' Tell your master, Peter Schlemihl, he will not see me here again. I am going to cross the sea; a favourable wind now calls all the passengers on board; but, in a year and a day I shall have the honour of paying him a visit; when, in all probability, I shall have a proposal to make to him of a very agreeable nature. Commend me to him most respectfully, with many thanks.' I inquired his name; but he said you would remember him."

"What sort of person was he?" cried I, in great emotion; and Bendel described the man in the grey coat feature by feature, word for word; in short, the very individual in search of whom he had been sent. "How unfortunate!" cried I bitterly; "it was himself." Scales, as it were, fell from Bendel's eyes. "Yes, it was he," cried he, "undoubtedly it was he; and fool, madman, that I was, I did not recognise him— I did not, and have betrayed my master!" He then broke out into a torrent of self-reproach; and his distress really excited my compassion. I endeavoured to console him, repeatedly assuring him that I entertained no doubt of his fidelity; and despatched him immediately to the wharf, to discover, if possible, some trace of the extraordinary being. But on that very morning many vessels which had been detained in port by contrary winds had set sail, all bound to different parts of the globe; and the grey man had disappeared like a shadow.

Chapter II

Of what use were wings to a man fast bound in chains of iron? They would but increase the horror of his despair. Like the dragon guarding his treasure, I remained cut off from all human intercourse, and starving amidst my very gold, for it gave me no pleasure: I anathematised it as the source of all my wretchedness.

Sole depository of my fearful secret, I trembled before the meanest of my attendants, whom, at the same time, I envied; for he possessed a shadow, and could venture to go out in the daytime; while I shut myself up in my room day and night, and indulged in all the bitterness of grief.

One individual, however, was daily pining away before my eyes—my faithful Bendel, who was the victim of silent self-reproach, tormenting himself with the idea that he had betrayed the confidence reposed in him by a good master, in failing to recognise the individual in quest of whom he had been sent, and with whom he had been led to believe that my melancholy fate was closely connected. Still, I had nothing to accuse him with, as I recognised in the occurrence the mysterious character of the unknown.

In order to leave no means untried, I one day despatched Bendel with a costly ring to the most celebrated artist in the town, desiring him to wait upon me. He came; and, dismissing the attendants, I secured the door, placing myself opposite to him, and, after extolling his art, with a heavy heart came to the point, first enjoining the strictest secrecy.

"For a person," said I, "who most unfortunately has lost his shadow, could you paint a false one?"

"Do you speak of the natural shadow?"

"Precisely so."

"But," he asked, "by what awkward negligence can a man have lost his shadow?"

"How it occurred," I answered, "is of no consequence; but it was in this manner"—(and here I uttered an unblushing falsehood)—"he was travelling in Russia last winter, and one bitterly cold day it froze so intensely, that his shadow remained so fixed to the ground, that it was found impossible to remove it."

"The false shadow that I might paint," said the artist, "would be liable to be lost on the slightest movement, particularly in a person who, from your account, cares so little about his shadow. A person without a shadow should keep out of the sun, that is the only safe and rational plan."

He rose and took his leave, casting so penetrating a look at me that I shrunk from it. I sank back in my chair, and hid my face in my hands.

In this attitude Bendel found me, and was about to withdraw silently and respectfully on seeing me in such a state of grief: looking up, overwhelmed with my sorrows, I felt that I must communicate them to him. "Bendel," I exclaimed, "Bendel, thou the only being who seest and respectest my grief too much to inquire into its cause—thou who seemest silently and sincerely to sympathise with me—come and share my confidence. The extent of my wealth I have not withheld from thee, neither will I conceal from thee the extent of my grief. Bendel! forsake me not. Bendel, you see me rich, free, beneficent; you fancy all the world in my power; yet you must have observed that I shun it, and avoid

all human intercourse. You think, Bendel, that the world and
I are at variance; and you your-self, perhaps, will abandon
me, when I acquaint you with this fearful secret. Bendel, I
am rich, free, generous; but, O God, I have *no shadow!*"

"No shadow!" exclaimed the faithful young man, tears
starting from his eyes. "Alas! that I am born to serve a master without a shadow!" He was silent, and again I hid my
face in my hands.

"Bendel," at last I tremblingly resumed, "you have now
my confidence; you may betray me—go—bear witness
against me!"

He seemed to be agitated with conflicting feelings; at
last he threw himself at my feet and seized my hand, which
he bathed with his tears. "No," he exclaimed; "whatever the world may say, I neither can nor will forsake my excellent master because he has lost his shadow. I will rather
do what is right than what may seem prudent. I will remain
with you—I will shade you with my own shadow—I will
assist you when I can—and when I cannot, I will weep with
you."

I fell upon his neck, astonished at sentiments so unusual; for it was very evident that he was not prompted by the
love of money.

My mode of life and my fate now became somewhat different. It is incredible with what provident foresight Bendel contrived to conceal my deficiency. Everywhere he was
before me and with me, providing against every contingen-
cy, and in cases of unlooked-for danger, flying to shield me
with his own shadow, for he was taller and stouter than myself. Thus I once more ventured among mankind, and began
to take a part in worldly affairs. I was compelled, indeed, to
affect certain peculiarities and whims; but in a rich man they
seem only appropriate; and so long as the truth was kept
concealed I enjoyed all the honour and respect which gold
could procure.

I now looked forward with more composure to the prom-
ised visit of the mysterious unknown at the expiration of the
year and a day.

I was very sensible that I could not venture to remain long in a place where I had once been seen without a shadow, and where I might easily be betrayed; and perhaps, too, I recollected my first introduction to Mr. John, and this was by no means a pleasing reminiscence. However, I wished just to make a trial here, that I might with greater ease and security visit some other place. But my vanity for some time withheld me, for it is in this quality of our race that the anchor takes the firmest hold.

Even the lovely Fanny, whom I again met in several places, without her seeming to recollect that she had ever seen me before, bestowed some notice on me; for wit and understanding were mine in abundance now. When I spoke, I was listened to; and I was at a loss to know how I had so easily acquired the art of commanding attention, and giving the tone to the conversation.

The impression which I perceived I had made upon this fair one completely turned my brain; and this was just what she wished. After that, I pursued her with infinite pains through every obstacle. My vanity was only intent on exciting hers to make a conquest of me; but although the intoxication disturbed my head, it failed to make the least impression on my heart.

But why detail to you the oft-repeated story which I have so often heard from yourself?

However, in the old and well-known drama in which I played so worn-out a part a catastrophe occurred of quite a peculiar nature, in a manner equally unexpected to her, to me, and to everybody.

One beautiful evening I had, according to my usual custom, assembled a party in a garden, and was walking arm-in-arm with Fanny at a little distance from the rest of the company, and pouring into her ear the usual well-turned phrases, while she was demurely gazing on vacancy, and now and then gently returning the pressure of my hand. The moon suddenly emerged from behind a cloud at our back. Fanny perceived only her own shadow before us. She started, looked at me with terror, and then again on the ground, in search of my shadow. All that was passing in her mind was so strangely depicted in her countenance, that I should have burst into a loud fit of laughter had I not suddenly felt my blood run cold within me. I suffered her to fall from my arm in a fainting-fit; shot with the rapidity of an arrow through the astonished guests, reached the gate, threw myself into the first conveyance I met with, and returned to the town, where this time, unfortunately, I had left the wary Bendel. He was alarmed on seeing me: one word explained all. Post-horses were immediately procured. I took with me none of my servants, one cunning knave only excepted, called Rascal, who had by his adroitness become very serviceable to me, and who at present knew nothing of what had occurred—I travelled thirty leagues that night; having left Bendel behind to discharge my servants, pay my debts, and bring me all that was necessary.

When he came up with me next day, I threw myself into his arms, vowing to avoid such follies and to be more careful for the future.

We pursued our journey uninterruptedly over the frontiers and mountains; and it was not until I had placed this lofty barrier between myself and the before-mentioned unlucky town that I was persuaded to recruit myself after my fatigues in a neighbouring and little-frequented watering-place.

I must now pass rapidly over one period of my history, on which how gladly would I dwell, could I conjure up your lively powers of delineation! But the vivid hues which are at your command, and which alone can give life and animation to the picture, have left no trace within me; and were I now to endeavour to recall the joys, the griefs, the pure and enchanting emotions, which once held such powerful dominion in my breast, it would be like striking a rock which yields no longer the living spring, and whose spirit has fled for ever. With what an altered aspect do those bygone days now present themselves to my gaze!

In this watering-place I acted an heroic character, badly studied; and being a novice on such a stage, I forgot my part before a pair of lovely blue eyes.

All possible means were used by the infatuated parents to conclude the bargain; and deception put an end to these usual artifices. And that is all—all.

The powerful emotions which once swelled my bosom seem now in the retrospect to be poor and insipid, nay, even terrible to me.

Alas, Minna! as I wept for thee the day I lost thee, so do I now weep that I can no longer retrace thine image in my soul.

Am I, then, so far advanced into the vale of years? O fatal effects of maturity! would that I could feel one throb, one emotion of former days of enchantment—alas, not one! a solitary being, tossed on the wild ocean of life—it is long since I drained thine enchanted cup to the dregs!

But to return to my narrative. I had sent Bendel to the little town with plenty of money to procure me a suitable habitation. He spent my gold profusely; and as he expressed himself rather reservedly concerning his distinguished master (for I did not wish to be named), the good people began to form rather extraordinary conjectures.

As soon as my house was ready for my reception, Bendel returned to conduct me to it. We set out on our journey. About a league from the town, on a sunny plain, we were stopped by a crowd of people, arrayed in holiday attire for some festival. The carriage stopped. Music, bells, cannons, were heard; and loud acclamations rang through the air.

Before the carriage now appeared in white dresses a chorus of maidens, all of extraordinary beauty; but one of them shone in resplendent loveliness, and eclipsed the rest as the sun eclipses the stars of night. She advanced from the midst of her companions, and, with a lofty yet winning air, blushingly knelt before me, presenting on a silken cushion a wreath, composed of laurel branches, the olive, and the rose, saying something respecting majesty, love, honour, &c., which I could not comprehend; but the sweet and silvery magic of her tones intoxicated my senses and my whole soul: it seemed as if some heavenly apparition were hovering over me. The chorus now began to sing the praises of a good sovereign, and the happiness of his subjects. All this, dear Chamisso, took place in the sun: she was kneeling two steps from me, and I, without a shadow, could not dart through the air, nor fall on my knees before the angelic being. Oh, what would I not now have given for a shadow! To conceal my shame, agony, and despair, I buried myself in the recesses of the carriage. Bendel at last thought of an expedient; he jumped out of the carriage. I called him back, and gave him out of the casket I had by me a rich diamond coronet, which had been intended for the lovely Fanny.

He stepped forward, and spoke in the name of his master, who, he said, was overwhelmed by so many demonstrations of respect, which he really could not accept as an honour—there must be some error; nevertheless he begged to express his thanks for the goodwill of the worthy townspeople. In the meantime Bendel had taken the wreath from the cushion, and laid the brilliant crown in its place. He then respectfully raised the lovely girl from the ground; and, at one sign, the clergy, magistrates, and all the deputations withdrew. The crowd separated to allow the horses to pass, and we pursued our way to the town at full gallop, through arches ornamented with flowers and branches of laurel. Salvos of artillery again were heard. The carriage stopped at my gate; I hastened through the crowd which curiosity had attracted to witness my arrival. Enthusiastic shouts resounded under my windows, from whence I showered gold amidst the people; and in the evening the whole town was illuminated. Still all remained a mystery to me, and I could not imagine for whom I had been taken. I sent Rascal out to make inquiry; and he soon obtained intelligence that the good King of Prussia was travelling through the country under the name of some count; that my aide-de-camp had been recognised, and that he had divulged the secret; that on acquiring the certainty that I would enter their town, their joy had known no bounds: however, as they perceived I was determined on preserving the strictest incognito, they felt how wrong they had been in too importunately seeking to withdraw the veil; but I had received them so condescendingly and so graciously, that they were sure I would forgive them. The whole affair was such capital amusement to the unprincipled Rascal, that he did his best to confirm the good people in their belief, while affecting to reprove them. He gave me a very comical account of the matter; and, seeing that I was amused by it, actually endeavoured to make a merit of his impudence.

Shall I own the truth? My vanity was flattered by having been mistaken for our revered sovereign. I ordered a banquet to be got ready for the following evening, under the trees before my house, and invited the whole town. The mysterious power of my purse, Bendel's exertions, and Rascal's ready invention, made the shortness of the time seem as nothing.

It was really astonishing how magnificently and beautifully everything was arranged in these few hours. Splendour and abundance vied with each other, and the lights were so carefully arranged that I felt quite safe: the zeal of my servants met every exigency and merited all praise.

Evening drew on, the guests arrived, and were presented to me. The word *majesty* was now dropped; but, with the deepest respect and humility, I was addressed as the *count*. What could I do? I accepted the title, and from that moment I was known as Count Peter. In the midst of all this festivity my soul pined for one individual. She came late—she who was the empress of the scene, and wore the emblem of sovereignty on her brow.

She modestly accompanied her parents, and seemed unconscious of her transcendent beauty.

The Ranger of the Forests, his wife, and daughter, were presented to me. I was at no loss to make myself agreeable to the parents; but before the daughter I stood like a well-scolded schoolboy, incapable of speaking a single word.

At length I hesitatingly entreated her to honour my banquet by presiding at it—an office for which her rare endowments pointed her out as admirably fitted. With a blush and an expressive glance she entreated to be excused; but, in still greater confusion than herself, I respectfully begged her to

accept the homage of the first and most devoted of her subjects, and one glance of the count was the same as a command to the guests, who all vied with each other in acting up
to the spirit of the noble host.

In her person majesty, innocence, and grace, in union
with beauty, presided over this joyous banquet. Minna's
happy parents were elated by the honours conferred upon their child. As for me, I abandoned myself to all the intoxication of delight: I sent for all the jewels, pearls, and
precious stones still left to me—the produce of my fatal
wealth—and, filling two vases, I placed them on the table, in
the name of the Queen of the banquet, to be divided among
her companions and the remainder of the ladies.

I ordered gold in the meantime to be showered down
without ceasing among the happy multitude.

Next morning Bendel told me in confidence that the sus-
picions he had long entertained of Rascal's honesty were
now reduced to a certainty; he had yesterday embezzled
many bags of gold.

"Never mind," said I; "let him enjoy his paltry booty. I
like to spend it; why should not he? Yesterday he, and all
the newly-engaged servants whom you had hired, served
me honourably, and cheerfully assisted me to enjoy the banquet."

No more was said on the subject. Rascal remained at the
head of my domestics. Bendel was my friend and confidant;
he had by this time become accustomed to look upon my
wealth as inexhaustible, without seeking to inquire into its
source. He entered into all my schemes, and effectually assisted me in devising methods of spending my money.

Of the pale, sneaking scoundrel—the unknown—Bendel only knew thus much, that he alone had power to release
me from the curse which weighed so heavily on me, and yet
that I stood in awe of him on whom all my hopes rested. Besides, I felt convinced that he had the means of discovering *me* under any circumstances, while he himself remained
concealed. I therefore abandoned my fruitless inquiries, and
patiently awaited the appointed day.

The magnificence of my banquet, and my deportment on the occasion, had but strengthened the credulous townspeople in their previous belief.

It appeared soon after, from accounts in the newspapers, that the whole history of the King of Prussia's fictitious journey originated in mere idle report. But a king I was, and a king I must remain by all means; and one of the richest and most royal, although people were at a loss to know where my territories lay.

The world has never had reason to lament the scarcity of monarchs, particularly in these days; and the good people, who had never yet seen a king, now fancied me to be first one, and then another, with equal success; and in the meanwhile I remained as before, Count Peter.

Among the visitors at this watering-place a merchant made his appearance, one who had become a bankrupt in order to enrich himself. He enjoyed the general good opinion; for he projected a shadow of respectable size, though of somewhat faint hue.

This man wished to show off in this place by means of his wealth, and sought to rival me. My purse soon enabled me to leave the poor devil far behind. To save his credit he became bankrupt again, and fled beyond the mountains; and thus I was rid of him. Many a one in this place was reduced to beggary and ruin through my means.

In the midst of the really princely magnificence and profusion, which carried all before me, my own style of living was very simple and retired. I had made it a point to observe the strictest precaution; and, with the exception of Bendel, no one was permitted, on any pretence whatever, to enter my private apartment. As long as the sun shone I remained shut up with him; and the Count was then said to be deeply occupied in his closet. The numerous couriers, whom I kept in constant attendance about matters of no importance, were supposed to be the bearers of my despatches. I only received company in the evening under the trees of my garden, or in my saloons, after Bendel's assurance of their being carefully and brilliantly lit up.

My walks, in which the Argus-eyed Bendel was constantly on the watch for me, extended only to the garden of
the forest-ranger, to enjoy the society of one who was dear
to me as my own existence.

Oh, my Chamisso! I trust thou hast not forgotten what
love is! I must here leave much to thine imagination. Minna was in truth an amiable and excellent maiden: her whole
soul was wrapped up in me, and in her lowly thoughts of
herself she could not imagine how she had deserved a single thought from me. She returned love for love with all the
full and youthful fervour of an innocent heart; her love was
a true woman's love, with all the devotion and total absence
of selfishness which is found only in woman; she lived but
in me, her whole soul being bound up in mine, regardless
what her own fate might be.

Yet I, alas, during those hours of wretchedness—hours
I would even now gladly recall—how often have I wept
on Bendel's bosom, when after the first mad whirlwind of
passion I reflected, with the keenest self-upbraidings, that
I, a shadowless man, had, with cruel selfishness, practised
a wicked deception, and stolen away the pure and angelic
heart of the innocent Minna!

At one moment I resolved to confess all to her; then that
I would fly for ever; then I broke out into a flood of bitter
tears, and consulted Bendel as to the means of meeting her
again in the forester's garden.

At times I flattered myself with great hopes from the near
approaching visit of the unknown; then wept again, because
I saw clear-ly on reflection that they would end in disappointment. I had made a calculation of the day fixed on by
the fearful being for our interview; for he had said in a year
and a day, and I depended on his word.

The parents were worthy old people, devoted to their only child; and our mutual affection was a circumstance so
overwhelming that they knew not how to act. They had never dreamed for a moment that the Count could bestow a
thought on their daughter; but such was the case—he loved
and was beloved. The pride of the mother might not have

led her to consider such an alliance quite impossible, but so extravagant an idea had never entered the contemplation of the sounder judgment of the old man. Both were satisfied of the sincerity of my love, and could but put up prayers to Heaven for the happiness of their child.

A letter which I received from Minna about that time has just fallen into my hands. Yes, these are the characters traced by her own hand. I will transcribe the letter:–

"I am indeed a weak, foolish girl to fancy that the friend I so tenderly love could give an instant's pain to his poor Minna! Oh no! thou art so good, so inexpressibly good! But do not misunderstand me. I will accept no sacrifice at thy hands—none whatever. Oh heavens! I should hate myself! No; thou hast made me happy, thou hast taught me to love thee.

"Go, then—let me not forget my destiny—Count Peter belongs not to me, but to the whole world; and oh! what pride for thy Minna to hear thy deeds proclaimed, and blessings invoked on thy idolised head! Ah! when I think of this, I could chide thee that thou shouldst for one instant forget thy high destiny for the sake of a simple maiden! Go, then; otherwise the reflection will pierce me. How blest I have been rendered by thy love! Perhaps, also, I have planted some flowers in the path of thy life, as I twined them in the wreath which I presented to thee.

"Go, then—fear not to leave me—you are too deeply seated in my heart—I shall die inexpressibly happy in thy love."

Conceive how these words pierced my soul, Chamisso!

I declared to her that I was not what I seemed—that, although a rich, I was an unspeakably miserable man—that a curse was on me, which must remain a secret, although the only one between us—yet that I was not without a hope of its being removed—that this poisoned every hour of my life—that I should plunge her with me into the abyss—she, the light and joy, the very soul of my existence. Then she wept because I was unhappy. Oh! Minna was all love and tenderness. To save me one tear she would gladly have sacrificed her life.

Yet she was far from comprehending the full meaning of my words. She still looked upon me as some proscribed prince or illustrious exile; and her vivid imagination had invested her lover with every lofty attribute.

One day I said to her, "Minna, the last day in next month will decide my fate, and perhaps change it for the better; if not, I would sooner die than render you miserable."

She laid her head on my shoulder to conceal her tears. "Should thy fate be changed," she said, "I only wish to know that thou art happy; if thy condition is an unhappy one, I will share it with thee, and assist thee to support it."

"Minna, Minna!" I exclaimed, "recall those rash words—those mad words which have escaped thy lips! Didst thou know the misery and curse—didst thou know who—what—thy lover—Seest thou not, my Minna, this convulsive shuddering which thrills my whole frame, and that there is a secret in my breast which you cannot penetrate?" She sank sobbing at my feet, and renewed her vows and entreaties.

Her father now entered, and I declared to him my intention to solicit the hand of his daughter on the first day of the month after the ensuing one. I fixed that time, I told him, because circumstances might probably occur in the interval materially to influence my future destiny; but my love for his daughter was unchangeable.

The good old man started at hearing such words from the mouth of Count Peter. He fell upon my neck, and rose again in the utmost confusion for having forgotten himself. Then he began to doubt, to ponder, and to scrutinise; and spoke of dowry, security, and future provision for his beloved child. I thanked him for having reminded me of all this, and told him it was my wish to remain in a country where I seemed to be beloved, and to lead a life free from anxiety. I then commissioned him to purchase the finest estate in the neighbourhood in the name of his daughter—for a father was the best person to act for his daughter in such a case—and to refer for payment to me. This occasioned him a good deal of trouble, as a stranger had everywhere anticipated him; but at last he made a purchase for about 150,000 pounds.

I confess this was but an innocent artifice to get rid of him, as I had frequently done before; for it must be confessed that he was somewhat tedious. The good mother was rather deaf, and not jealous, like her husband, of the honour of conversing with the Count.

The happy party pressed me to remain with them longer this evening. I dared not—I had not a moment to lose. I saw the rising moon streaking the horizon—my hour was come.

Next evening I went again to the forester's garden. I had wrapped myself closely up in my cloak, slouched my hat over my eyes, and advanced towards Minna. As she raised her head and looked at me, she started involuntarily. The apparition of that dreadful night in which I had been seen without a shadow was now standing distinctly before me—it was she herself. Had she recognised me? She was silent and thoughtful. I felt an oppressive load at my heart. I rose from my seat. She laid her head on my shoulder, still silent and in tears. I went away.

I now found her frequently weeping. I became more and more melancholy. Her parents were beyond expression happy. The eventful day approached, threatening and heavy, like a thundercloud. The evening preceding arrived. I could scarcely breathe. I had carefully filled a large chest with gold, and sat down to await the appointed time—the twelfth hour—it struck.

Now I remained with my eyes fixed on the hand of the clock, counting the seconds—the minutes—which struck me to the heart like daggers. I started at every sound—at last daylight appeared. The leaden hours passed on—morning—evening—night came. Hope was fast fading away as the hand advanced. It struck eleven—no one appeared—the last minutes—the first and last stroke of the twelfth hour died away. I sank back in my bed in an agony of weeping. In the morning I should, shadowless as I was, claim the hand of my beloved Minna. A heavy sleep towards daylight closed my eyes.

Chapter III

It was yet early, when I was suddenly awoke by voices in hot dispute in my antechamber. I listened. Bendel was forbidding Rascal to enter my room, who swore he would receive no orders from his equals, and insisted on forcing his way. The faithful Bendel reminded him that if such words reached his master's ears, he would turn him out of an excellent place. Rascal threatened to strike him if he persisted in refusing his entrance.

By this time, having half dressed myself, I angrily threw open the door, and addressing my-self to Rascal, inquired what he meant by such disgraceful conduct. He drew back a couple of steps, and coolly answered, "Count Peter, may I beg most respectfully that you will favour me with a sight of your shadow? The sun is now shining brightly in the court below."

I stood as if struck by a thunderbolt, and for some time was unable to speak. At last, I asked him how a servant could dare to behave so towards his master. He interrupted me by saying, quite coolly, "A servant may be a very honourable man, and unwilling to serve a shadowless master— I request my dismissal."

I felt that I must adopt a softer tone, and replied, "But, Rascal, my good fellow, who can have put such strange ideas into your head? How can you imagine—"

He again interrupted me in the same tone—"People say you have no shadow. In short, let me see your shadow, or give me my dismissal."

Bendel, pale and trembling, but more collected than myself, made a sign to me. I had recourse to the all-powerful influence of gold. But even gold had lost its power—Rascal threw it at my feet: "From a shadowless man," he said, "I will take nothing."

Turning his back upon me, and putting on his hat, he then slowly left the room, whistling a tune. I stood, with Bendel, as if petrified, gazing after him.

With a deep sigh and a heavy heart I now prepared to keep my engagement, and to appear in the forester's garden like a criminal before his judge. I entered by the shady arbour, which had received the name of Count Peter's arbour, where we had appointed to meet. The mother advanced with a cheerful air; Minna sat fair and beautiful as the early snow of autumn reposing on the departing flowers, soon to be dissolved and lost in the cold stream.

The ranger, with a written paper in his hand, was walking up and down in an agitated manner, and struggling to suppress his feelings—his usually unmoved countenance being one moment flushed, and the next perfectly pale. He came forward as I entered, and, in a faltering voice, requested a private conversation with me. The path by which he requested me to follow him led to an open spot in the garden, where the sun was shining. I sat down. A long silence ensued, which even the good woman herself did not venture to break. The ranger, in an agitated manner, paced up and down with unequal steps. At last he stood still; and glancing over the paper he held in his hand, he said, addressing me with a penetrating look,

"Count Peter, do you know one Peter Schlemihl?" I was silent.

"A man," he continued, "of excellent character and extraordinary endowments."

He paused for an answer.—"And supposing I myself were that very man?"

"You!" he exclaimed, passionately; "he has lost his shadow!"

"Oh, my suspicion is true!" cried Minna; "I have long known it—he has no shadow!" And she threw herself into her mother's arms, who, convulsively clasping her to her bosom, reproached her for having so long, to her hurt, kept such a secret. But, like the fabled Arethusa, her tears, as from a fountain, flowed more abundantly, and her sobs increased at my approach.

"And so," said the ranger fiercely, "you have not scrupled, with unparalleled shamelessness, to deceive both her and me; and you pretended to love her, forsooth—her whom you have reduced to the state in which you now see her. See how she weeps!—Oh, shocking, shocking!"

By this time I had lost all presence of mind; and I answered, confusedly, "After all, it is but a shadow, a mere shadow, which a man can do very well without; and really it is not worth the while to make all this noise about such a trifle." Feeling the groundlessness of what I was saying, I ceased, and no one condescended to reply. At last I added, "What is lost to-day may be found to-morrow."

"Be pleased, sir," continued the ranger, in great wrath— "be pleased to explain how you have lost your shadow."

Here again an excuse was ready: "A boor of a fellow," said I, "one day trod so rudely on my shadow that he tore a large hole in it. I sent it to be repaired—for gold can do wonders—and yesterday I expected it home again."

"Very well," answered the ranger. "You are a suitor for my daughter's hand, and so are others. As a father, I am bound to provide for her. I will give you three days to seek your shadow. Return to me in the course of that time with a well-fitted shadow, and you shall receive a hearty welcome; otherwise, on the fourth day—remember, on the fourth day—my daughter becomes the wife of another."

I now attempted to say one word to Minna; but, sobbing more violently, she clung still closer to her mother, who made a sign for me to withdraw. I obeyed; and now the world seemed shut out from me for ever.

Having escaped from the affectionate care of Bendel, I now wandered wildly through the neighbouring woods and meadows. Drops of anguish fell from my brow, deep groans burst from my bosom—frenzied despair raged within me.

I knew not how long this had lasted, when I felt myself seized by the sleeve on a sunny heath. I stopped, and looking up, beheld the grey-coated man, who appeared to have run himself out of breath in pursuing me. He immediately began:

"I had," said he, "appointed this day; but your impatience anticipated it. All, however, may yet be right. Take my advice—redeem your shadow, which is at your command, and return immediately to the ranger's garden, where you will be well received, and all the past will seem a mere joke. As for Rascal—who has betrayed you in order to pay his

addresses to Minna—leave him to me; he is just a fit subject for me."

I stood like one in a dream. "This day?" I considered
again. He was right—I had made a mistake of a day. I felt
in my bosom for the purse. He perceived my intention, and
drew back.

"No, Count Peter; the purse is in good hands—pray keep
it." I gazed at him with looks of astonishment and inquiry. "I
only beg a trifle as a token of remembrance. Be so good as to
sign this memorandum." On the parchment, which he held
out to me, were these words: —"By virtue of this present,
to which I have appended my signature, I hereby bequeath
my soul to the holder, after its natural separation from my
body."

I gazed in mute astonishment alternately at the paper and
the grey unknown. In the meantime he had dipped a new
pen in a drop of blood which was issuing from a scratch
in my hand just made by a thorn. He presented it to me.
"Who are you?" at last I exclaimed. "What can it signify?"
he answered; "do you not perceive who I am? A poor devil—a sort of scholar and philosopher, who obtains but poor
thanks from his friends for his admirable arts, and whose
only amusement on earth consists in his small experiments.
But just sign this; to the right, exactly underneath—Peter
Schlemihl."

I shook my head, and replied, "Excuse me, sir; I cannot
sign that."

"Cannot!" he exclaimed; "and why not?"

"Because it appears to me a hazardous thing to exchange
my soul for my shadow."

"Hazardous!" he exclaimed, bursting into a loud laugh.
"And, pray, may I be allowed to inquire what sort of a thing
your soul is?—have you ever seen it?—and what do you
mean to do with it after your death? You ought to think
yourself fortunate in meeting with a customer who, during your life, in exchange for this infinitely-minute quanti-
ty, this galvanic principle, this polarised agency, or whatever other foolish name you may give it, is willing to bestow

on you something substantial—in a word, your own identical shadow, by virtue of which you will obtain your beloved Minna, and arrive at the accomplishment of all your wishes; or do you prefer giving up the poor young girl to the power of that contemptible scoundrel Rascal? Nay, you shall behold her with your own eyes. Come here; I will lend you an invisible cap (he drew something out of his pocket), and we will enter the ranger's garden unseen."

I must confess that I felt excessively ashamed to be thus laughed at by the grey stranger. I detested him from the very bottom of my soul; and I really believe this personal antipathy, more than principle or previously-formed opinion, restrained me from purchasing my shadow, much as I stood in need of it, at such an expense. Besides, the thought was insupportable, of making this proposed visit in his society. To behold this hateful sneak, this mocking fiend, place himself between me and my beloved, between our torn and bleeding hearts, was too revolting an idea to be entertained for a moment. I considered the past as irrevocable, my own misery as inevitable; and turning to the grey man, I said, "I have exchanged my shadow for this very extraordinary purse, and I have sufficiently repented it. For Heaven's sake, let the transaction be declared null and void!" He shook his head; and his countenance assumed an expression of the most sinister cast. I continued, "I will make no exchange whatever, even for the sake of my shadow, nor will I sign the paper. It follows, also, that the incognito visit you propose to me would afford you far more entertainment than it could possibly give me. Accept my excuses, therefore; and, since it must be so, let us part."

"I am sorry, Mr. Schlemihl, that you thus obstinately persist in rejecting my friendly offer. Perhaps, another time, I may be more fortunate. Farewell! May we shortly meet again! But, a propos, allow me to show you that I do not undervalue my purchase, but preserve it carefully."

So saying, he drew my shadow out of his pocket; and shaking it cleverly out of its folds, he stretched it out at his feet in the sun—so that he stood between two obedient shadows, his own and mine, which was compelled to follow and comply with his every movement.

On again beholding my poor shadow after so long a separation, and seeing it degraded to so vile a bondage at the very time that I was so unspeakably in want of it, my heart was ready to burst, and I wept bitterly. The detested wretch stood exulting over his prey, and unblushingly renewed his proposal. "One stroke of your pen, and the unhappy Minna is rescued from the clutches of the villain Rascal, and transferred to the arms of the high-born Count Peter—merely a stroke of your pen!"

My tears broke out with renewed violence; but I turned away from him, and made a sign for him to be gone.

Bendel, whose deep solicitude had induced him to come in search of me, arrived at this very moment. The good and faithful creature, on seeing me weeping, and that a shadow (evidently mine) was in the power of the mysterious unknown, determined to rescue it by force, should that be necessary; and disdaining to use any finesse, he desired him directly, and without any disputing, to restore my property. Instead of a reply, the grey man turned his back on the worthy fellow, and was making off. But Bendel raised his buckthorn stick; and following close upon him, after repeated commands, but in vain, to restore the shadow, he made him feel the whole force of his powerful arm. The grey man, as if accustomed to such treatment, held down his head, slouched his shoulders, and, with soft and noiseless steps, pursued his way over the heath, carrying with him my shadow, and also my faithful servant. For a long time I heard hollow sounds ringing through the waste, until at last they died away in the distance, and I was again left to solitude and misery.

Alone on the wild heath, I disburdened my heart of an insupportable load by giving free vent to my tears. But I saw no bounds, no relief, to my surpassing wretchedness; and I drank in the fresh poison which the mysterious stranger had poured into my wounds with a furious avidity. As I retraced in my mind the loved image of my Minna, and depicted her sweet countenance all pale and in tears, such as I had beheld her in my late disgrace, the bold and sarcastic visage of Rascal would ever and anon thrust itself between us. I hid my face, and fled rapidly over the plains; but the horrible vision unrelentingly pursued me, till at last I sank breathless on the ground, and bedewed it with a fresh torrent of tears—and all this for a shadow!—a shadow which one stroke of the pen would repurchase. I pondered on the singular proposal, and on my hesitation to comply with it. My mind was confused—I had lost the power of judging or comprehending. The day was waning apace. I satisfied the cravings of hunger with a few wild fruits, and quenched my thirst at a neighbouring stream. Night came on; I threw myself down under a tree, and was awoke by the damp morning air from an uneasy sleep, in which I had fancied myself struggling in the agonies of death. Bendel had certainly lost all trace of me, and I was glad of it. I did not wish to return among my fellow-creatures—I shunned them as the hunted deer flies before its pursuers. Thus I passed three melancholy days.

I found myself on the morning of the fourth on a sandy plain, basking in the rays of the sun, and sitting on a fragment of rock; for it was sweet to enjoy the genial warmth of which I had so long been deprived. Despair still preyed on my heart. Suddenly a slight sound startled me; I looked round, prepared to fly, but saw no one. On the sunlit sand before me flitted the shadow of a man not unlike my own; and wandering about alone, it seemed to have lost its master. This sight powerfully excited me. "Shadow!" thought I, "art thou in search of thy master? in me thou shalt find him." And I sprang forward to seize it, fancying that could I succeed in treading so exactly in its traces as to step in its footmarks, it would attach itself to me, and in time become accustomed to me, and follow all my movements.

The shadow, as I moved, took to flight, and I commenced a hot chase after the airy fugitive, solely excited by the hope of being delivered from my present dreadful situation; the bare idea inspired me with fresh strength and vigour.

The shadow now fled towards a distant wood, among whose shades I must necessarily have lost it. Seeing this, my heart beat wild with fright, my ardour increased and lent wings to my speed. I was evidently gaining on the shadow—I came nearer and nearer—I was within reach of it, when it suddenly stopped and turned towards me. Like a lion darting on its prey, I made a powerful spring and fell unexpectedly upon a hard substance. Then followed, from an invisible hand, the most terrible blows in the ribs that anyone ever received. The effect of my terror made me endeavour convulsively to strike and grasp at the unseen object before me. The rapidity of my motions brought me to the ground, where I lay stretched out with a man under me, whom I held tight, and who now became visible.

The whole affair was now explained. The man had undoubtedly possessed the bird's nest which communicates its charm of invisibility to its possessor, though not equally so to his shadow; and this nest he had now thrown away. I looked all round, and soon discovered the shadow of this invisible nest.

I sprang towards it, and was fortunate enough to seize the precious booty, and immediately became invisible and shadowless.

The moment the man regained his feet he looked all round over the wide sunny plain to discover his fortunate vanquisher, but could see neither him nor his shadow, the latter seeming particularly to be the object of his search: for previous to our encounter he had not had leisure to observe that I was shadowless, and he could not be aware of it. Becoming convinced that all traces of me were lost, he began to tear his hair, and give himself up to all the frenzy of despair. In the meantime, this newly acquired treasure communicated to me both the ability and the desire to mix again among mankind.

I was at a loss for a pretext to vindicate this unjust robbery—or, rather, so deadened had I become, I felt no need of a pretext; and in order to dissipate every idea of the kind, I hastened on, regardless of the unhappy man, whose fearful lamentations long resounded in my ears. Such, at the time, were my impressions of all the circumstances of this affair.

I now ardently desired to return to the ranger's garden, in order to ascertain in person the truth of the information communicated by the odious unknown; but I knew not where I was, until, ascending an eminence to take a survey of the surrounding country, I perceived, from its summit, the little town and the gardens almost at my feet. My heart beat violently, and tears of a nature very different from those I had lately shed filled my eyes. I should, then, once more behold her!

Anxiety now hastened my steps. Unseen I met some peasants coming from the town; they were talking of me, of Rascal, and of the ranger. I would not stay to listen to their conversation, but proceeded on. My bosom thrilled with expectation as I entered the garden. At this moment I heard something like a hollow laugh which caused me involuntarily to shudder. I cast a rapid glance around, but could see no one. I passed on; presently I fancied I heard the sound of footsteps close to me, but no one was within sight. My ears must have deceived me.

It was early; no one was in Count Peter's bower—the gardens were deserted. I traversed all the well-known paths, and penetrated even to the dwelling-house itself. The same rustling sound became now more and more audible. With anguished feelings I sat down on a seat placed in the sunny space before the door, and actually felt some invisible fiend take a place by me, and heard him utter a sarcastic laugh. The key was turned in the door, which was opened. The forest-master appeared with a paper in his hand. Suddenly my head was, as it were, enveloped in a mist. I looked up, and, oh horror! the grey-coated man was at my side, peering in my face with a satanic grin. He had extended the mist-cap he wore over my head. His shadow and my own were lying together at his feet in perfect amity. He kept twirling in his hand the well-known parchment with an air of indifference; and while the ranger, absorbed in thought, and intent upon his paper, paced up and down the arbour, my tormentor confidentially leaned towards me, and whispered, "So, Mr. Schlemihl, you have at length accepted my invitation;

and here we sit, two heads under one hood, as the saying is. Well, well, all in good time. But now you can return me my bird's nest—you have no further occasion for it; and I am sure you are too honourable a man to withhold it from me. No need of thanks, I assure you; I had infinite pleasure in lending it to you." He took it out of my unresisting hand, put it into his pocket, and then broke into so loud a laugh at my expense, that the forest-master turned round, startled at the sound. I was petrified. "You must acknowledge," he continued, "that in our position a hood is much more con-venient. It serves to conceal not only a man, but his shadow, or as many shadows as he chooses to carry. I, for instance, to-day bring two, you perceive." He laughed again. "Take notice, Schlemihl, that what a man refuses to do with a good grace in the first instance, he is always in the end compelled to do. I am still of opinion that you ought to redeem your shadow and claim your bride (for it is yet time); and as to Rascal, he shall dangle at a rope's end—no difficult matter, so long as we can find a bit. As a mark of friendship I will give you my cap into the bargain."

The mother now came out, and the following conver-sation took place: "What is Minna doing?" "She is weeping." "Silly child! what good can that do?" "None, certainly; but it is so soon to bestow her hand on another. O husband, you are too harsh to your poor child." "No, wife; you view things in a wrong light. When she finds herself the wife of a wealthy and honourable man, her tears will soon cease; she will waken out of a dream, as it were, happy and grateful to Heaven and to her parents, as you will see." "Heaven grant it may be so!" replied the wife. "She has, indeed, now con-siderable property; but after the noise occasioned by her un-lucky affair with that adventurer, do you imagine that she is likely soon to meet with so advantageous a match as Mr. Rascal? Do you know the extent of Mr. Rascal's influence and wealth? Why, he has purchased with ready money, in this country, six millions of landed property, free from all encumbrances. I have had all the documents in my hands. It was he who outbid me everywhere when I was about to make a desirable purchase; and, besides, he has bills on Mr. Thomas John's house to the amount of three millions and a half." "He must have been a prodigious thief!" "How foolishly you talk! he wisely saved where others squandered their property." "A mere livery-servant!" "Nonsense! he has at all events an unexceptionable shadow." "True, but . . . "

While this conversation was passing, the grey-coated man looked at me with a satirical smile.

The door opened, and Minna entered, leaning on the arm of her female attendant, silent tears flowing down her fair but pallid face. She seated herself in the chair which had been placed for her under the lime-trees, and her father took a stool by her side. He gently raised her hand; and as her tears flowed afresh, he addressed her in the most affectionate manner

"My own dear, good child—my Minna—will act reasonably, and not afflict her poor old father, who only wishes to make her happy. My dearest child, this blow has shaken you—dreadfully, I know it; but you have been saved, as by a miracle, from a miserable fate, my Minna. You loved the unworthy villain most tenderly before his treachery was discovered: I feel all this, Minna; and far be it from me to reproach you for it—in fact, I myself loved him so long as I considered him to be a person of rank: you now see yourself how differently it has turned out. Every dog has a shadow; and the idea of my child having been on the eve of uniting herself to a man who... but I am sure you will think no more of him. A suitor has just appeared for you in the person of a man who does not fear the sun—an honourable man—no prince indeed, but a man worth ten millions of golden ducats sterling—a sum nearly ten times larger than your fortune consists of—a man, too, who will make my dear child happy—nay, do not oppose me—be my own good, dutiful child—allow your loving father to provide for you, and to dry up these tears. Promise to bestow your hand on Mr. Rascal. Speak my child: will you not?"

Minna could scarcely summon strength to reply that she had now no longer any hopes or desires on earth, and that she was entirely at her father's disposal. Rascal was therefore immediately sent for, and entered the room with his usual forwardness; but Minima in the meantime had swooned away.

My detested companion looked at me indignantly, and whispered, "Can you endure this? Have you no blood in your veins?" He instantly pricked my finger, which bled. "Yes, positively," he exclaimed, "you have some blood left!— come, sign." The parchment and pen were in my hand!

Chapter IV

I submit myself to thy judgment, my dear Chamisso; I do not seek to bias it. I have long been a rigid censor of myself, and nourished at my heart the worm of remorse. This critical moment of my life is ever present to my soul, and I dare only cast a hesitating glance at it, with a deep sense of humiliation and grief. Ah, my dear friend, he who once permits himself thoughtlessly to deviate but one step from the right road, will imperceptibly find himself involved in various intricate paths, all leading him farther and farther astray. In vain he beholds the guiding-stars of Heaven shining before him. No choice is left him—he must descend the precipice, and offer himself up a sacrifice to his fate. After the false step which I had rashly made, and which entailed a curse upon me, I had, in the wantonness of passion, entangled one in my fate who had staked all her happiness upon me. What was left for me to do in a case where I had brought another into misery, but to make a desperate leap in the dark to save her ?—the last, the only means of rescue presented itself. Think not so meanly of me, Chamisso, as to imagine that I would have shrunk from any sacrifice on my part. In such a case it would have been but a poor ransom. No, Chamisso; but my whole soul was filled with unconquerable hatred to the cringing knave and his crooked ways. I might be doing him injustice; but I shuddered at the bare idea of entering into any fresh compact with him. But here a circumstance took place which entirely changed the face of things . . .

I know not whether to ascribe it to excitement of mind, exhaustion of physical strength (for during the last few days I had scarcely tasted anything), or the antipathy I felt to the society of my fiendish companion; but just as I was about to sign the fatal paper, I fell into a deep swoon, and remained for a long time as if dead. The first sounds which greeted my ear on recovering my consciousness were those of cursing and imprecation; I opened my eyes—it was dusk; my hateful companion was overwhelming me with reproaches. "Is not this behaving like an old woman? Come, rise up, and finish quickly what you were going to do; or perhaps you have changed your determination, and prefer to lie groaning there?"

I raised myself with difficulty from the ground and gazed around me without speaking a word. It was late in the evening, and I heard strains of festive music proceeding from the ranger's brilliantly illuminated house; groups of company were lounging about the gardens; two persons approached, and seating themselves on the bench I had lately occupied, began to converse on the subject of the marriage which had taken place that morning between the wealthy Mr. Rascal and Minima. All was then over.

I tore off the cap which rendered me invisible; and my companion having disappeared, I plunged in silence into the thickest gloom of the grove, rapidly passed Count Peter's bower towards the entrance-gate; but my tormentor still haunted me, and loaded me with reproaches. "And is this all the gratitude I am to expect from you, Mr. Schlemihl—you, whom I have been watching all the weary day, until you should recover from your nervous attack? What a fool's part I have been enacting! It is of no use flying from me, Mr. Perverse—we are inseparable—you have my gold, I have your shadow; this exchange deprives us both of peace. Did you ever hear of a man's shadow leaving him?—yours follows me until you receive it again into favour, and thus free me from it. Disgust and weariness sooner or later will compel you to do what you should have done gladly at first. In vain you strive with fate!"

He continued unceasingly in the same tone, uttering constant sarcasms about the gold and the shadow, till I was completely bewildered. To fly from him was impossible. I had pursued my way through the empty streets towards my own house, which I could scarcely recognise—the windows were broken to pieces, no light was visible, the doors were shut, and the bustle of domestics had ceased. My companion burst into a loud laugh. "Yes, yes," said he, "you see the state of things: however, you will find your friend Bendel at home; he was sent back the other day so fatigued, that I assure you he has never left the house since. He will have a fine story to tell! So I wish you a very good night—may we shortly meet again!"

I had repeatedly rung the bell: at last a light appeared; and Bendel inquired from within who was there. The poor fellow could scarcely contain himself at the sound of my voice. The door flew open, and we were locked in each other's arms. I found him sadly changed; he was looking ill and feeble. I, too, was altered; my hair had become quite grey. He conducted me through the desolate apartments to an inner room, which had escaped the general wreck. After partaking of some refreshment, we seated ourselves; and, with fresh lamentations, he began to tell me that the grey withered old man whom he had met with my shadow had insensibly led him such a zig-zag race, that he had lost all traces of me, and at last sank down exhausted with fatigue; that, unable to find me, he had returned home, when, shortly after the mob, at Rascal's instigation, assembled violently before the house, broke the windows, and by all sorts of excesses completely satiated their fury. Thus had they treated their benefactor. My servants had fled in all directions. The police had banished me from the town as a suspicious character, and granted me an interval of twenty-four hours to leave the territory. Bendel added many particulars as to the information I had already obtained respecting Rascal's wealth and marriage. This villain, it seems—who was the author of all the measures taken against me—became possessed of my secret nearly from the beginning, and, tempted by the love of money, had supplied himself with a key to my chest, and from that time had been laying the foundation of his present wealth. Bendel related all this with many tears, and wept for joy that I was once more safely restored to him, after all his fears and anxieties for me. In me, however, such a state of things only awoke despair.

My dreadful fate now stared me in the face in all its gigantic and unchangeable horror. The source of tears was exhausted within me; no groans escaped my breast; but with cool indifference I bared my unprotected head to the blast. "Bendel," said I, "you know my fate; this heavy visitation is a punishment for my early sins: but as for thee, my innocent friend, I can no longer permit thee to share my destiny. I will depart this very night—saddle me a horse—I will set out alone. Remain here, Bendel—I insist upon it: there must be some chests of gold still left in the house—take them, they are thine. I shall be a restless and solitary wanderer on the face of the earth; but should better days arise, and fortune once more smile propitiously on me, then I will not forget thy steady fidelity; for in hours of deep distress thy faithful bosom has been the depository of my sorrows." With a bursting heart, the worthy Bendel prepared to obey this last command of his master; for I was deaf to all his arguments and blind to his tears. My horse was brought—I pressed my weeping friend to my bosom—threw myself into the saddle, and, under the friendly shades of night, quitted this sepulchre of my existence, indifferent which road my horse should take; for now on this side the grave I had neither wishes, hopes, nor fears.

After a short time I was joined by a traveller on foot, who, after walking for a while by the side of my horse, observed that as we both seemed to be travelling the same road, he should beg my permission to lay his cloak on the horse's back behind me, to which I silently assented. He thanked me with easy politeness for this trifling favour, praised my horse, and then took occasion to extol the happiness and the power of the rich, and fell, I scarcely know how, into

a sort of conversation with himself, in which I merely acted the part of listener. He unfolded his views of human life
and of the world, and, touching on metaphysics, demanded
an answer from that cloudy science to the question of questions—the answer that should solve all mysteries. He de-
duced one problem from another in a very lucid manner, and
then proceeded to their solution.

You may remember, my dear friend, that after having run
through the school-philo-sophy, I became sensible of my
unfitness for metaphysical speculations, and therefore totally abstained from engaging in them. Since then I have ac-
quiesced in some things, and abandoned all hope of comprehending others; trusting, as you advised me, to my own
plain sense and the voice of conscience to direct and, if possible, maintain me in the right path.

Now this skilful rhetorician seemed to me to expend
great skill in rearing a firmly-constructed edifice, tower-
ing aloft on its own self-supported basis, but resting on, and
upheld by, some internal principle of necessity. I regretted
in it the total absence of what I desired to find; and thus it
seemed a mere work of art, serving only by its elegance and
exquisite finish to captivate the eye. Nevertheless, I listened
with pleasure to this eloquently gifted man, who diverted
my attention from my own sorrows to the speaker; and he
would have secured my entire acquiescence if he had ap-
pealed to my heart as well as to my judgment.

In the meantime the hours had passed away, and morning had already dawned imperceptibly in the horizon; looking up, I shuddered as I beheld in the east all those splendid
hues that announce the rising sun. At this hour, when all natural shadows are seen in their full proportions, not a fence or
a shelter of any kind could I descry in this open country, and
I was not alone! I cast a glance at my companion, and shuddered again—it was the man in the grey coat himself! He
laughed at my surprise, and said, without giving me time to
speak: "You see, according to the fashion of this world, mutual convenience binds us together for a time: there is plenty of time to think of parting. The road here along the moun-

tain, which perhaps has escaped your notice, is the only one that you can prudently take; into the valley you dare not descend—the path over the mountain would but reconduct you to the town which you have left—my road, too, lies this way. I perceive you change colour at the rising sun—I have no objections to let you have the loan of your shadow during our journey, and in return you may not be indisposed to tolerate my society. You have now no Bendel; but I will act for him. I regret that you are not overfond of me; but that need not prevent you from accepting my poor services. The devil is not so black as he is painted. Yesterday you provoked me, I own; but now that is all forgotten, and you must confess I have this day succeeded in beguiling the wearisomeness of your journey. Come, take your shadow, and make trial of it."

The sun had risen, and we were meeting with passengers; so I reluctantly consented. With a smile, he immediately let my shadow glide down to the ground; and I beheld it take its place by that of my horse, and gaily trot along with me. My feelings were anything but pleasant. I rode through groups of country people, who respectfully made way for the well-mounted stranger. Thus I proceeded, occasionally stealing a sidelong glance with a beating heart from my horse at the shadow once my own, but now, alas, accepted as a loan from a stranger, or rather a fiend. He moved on carelessly at my side, whistling a song. He being on foot, and I on horseback, the temptation to hazard a silly project occurred to me; so, suddenly turning my bridle, I set spurs to my horse, and at full gallop struck into a by-path; but my shadow, on the sudden movement of my horse, glided away, and stood on the road quietly awaiting the approach of its legal owner. I was obliged to return abashed towards the grey man; but he very coolly finished his song, and with a laugh set my shadow to rights again, reminding me that it was at my option to have it irrevocably fixed to me, by purchasing it on just and equitable terms. "I hold you," said he, "by the shadow; and you seek in vain to get rid of me. A rich man like you requires a shadow, unquestionably; and you are to blame for not having seen this sooner."

I now continued my journey on the same road; every convenience and even luxury of life was mine; I moved about in peace and freedom, for I possessed a shadow, though a borrowed one; and all the respect due to wealth was paid to me. But a deadly disease preyed on my heart. My extraordinary companion, who gave himself out to be the humble attendant of the richest individual in the world, was remarkable for his dexterity; in short, his singular address and promptitude admirably fitted him to be the very beau ideal of a rich man's lacquey. But he never stirred from my side, and tormented me with constant assurances that a day would most certainly come when, if it were only to get rid of him, I should gladly comply with his terms, and redeem my shadow. Thus he became as irksome as he was hateful to me. I really stood in awe of him—I had placed myself in his power. Since he had effected my return to the pleasures of the world, which I had resolved to shun, he had the perfect mastery of me. His eloquence was irresistible, and at times I almost thought he was in the right. A shadow is indeed necessary to a man of fortune; and if I chose to maintain the position in which he had placed me, there was only one means of doing so. But on one point I was immovable: since I had sacrificed my love for Minna, and thereby blighted the happiness of my whole life, I would not now, for all the shadows in the universe be induced to sign away my soul to this being—I knew not how it might end.

One day we were sitting by the entrance of a cavern, much visited by strangers, who ascended the mountain: the rushing noise of a subterranean torrent resounded from the fathomless abyss, the depths of which exceeded all calculation. He was, according to his favourite custom, employing all the powers of his lavish fancy, and all the charm of the most brilliant colouring, to depict to me what I might effect in the world by virtue of my purse, when once I had recovered my shadow. With my elbows resting on my knees, I kept my face concealed in my hands, and listened to the false fiend, my heart torn between the temptation and my determined opposition to it. Such indecision I could no longer endure, and resolved on one decisive effort.

"You seem to forget," said I, "that I tolerate your presence only on certain conditions, and that I am to retain perfect freedom of action."

"You have but to command, I depart," was all his reply.

The threat was familiar to me; I was silent. He then began to fold up my shadow. I turned pale, but allowed him to continue. A long silence ensued, which he was the first to break.

"You cannot endure me, Mr Schlemihl—you hate me— I am aware of it—but why?—is it, perhaps, because you attacked me on the open plain, in order to rob me of my invisible bird's nest? or is it because you thievishly endeavoured to seduce away the shadow with which I had entrusted you—my own property—confiding implicitly in your honour! I, for my part, have no dislike to you. It is perfectly natural that you should avail yourself of every means, presented either by cunning or force, to promote your own interests. That your principles also should be of the strictest sort, and your intentions of the most honourable description,—these are fancies with which I have nothing to do; I do not pretend to such strictness myself. Each of us is free, I to act, and you to think, as seems best. Did I ever seize you by the throat, to tear out of your body that valuable soul I so ardently wish to possess? Did I ever set my servant to attack you, to get back my purse, or attempt to run off with it from you?"

I had not a word to reply.

"Well, well," he exclaimed, "you detest me, and I know it; but I bear you no malice on that account. We must part— that is clear; also I must say that you begin to be very tiresome to me. Once more let me advise you to free yourself entirely from my trouble-some presence by the purchase of your shadow."

I held out the purse to him.

"No, Mr. Schlemihl; not at that price."

With a deep sigh, I said, "Be it so, then; let us part, I entreat; cross my path no more. There is surely room enough in the world for us both."

Laughing, he replied, "I go; but just allow me to inform you how you may at any time recall me whenever you have a mind to see your most humble servant: you have only to shake your purse, the sound of the gold will bring me to you in an instant. In this world every one consults his own advantage; but you see I have thought of yours, and clearly confer upon you a new power. Oh this purse! it would still prove a powerful bond between us, had the moth begun to devour your shadow.—But enough: you hold me by my gold, and may command your servant at any distance. You know that I can be very serviceable to my friends; and that the rich are my peculiar care—this you have observed. As to your shadow, allow me to say, you can only redeem it on one condition."

Recollections of former days came over me; and I hastily asked him if he had obtained Mr. Thomas John's signature.

He smiled, and said, "It was by no means necessary from so excellent a friend."

"Where is he? for God's sake tell me: I insist upon knowing."

With some hesitation, he put his hand into his pocket; and drew out the altered and pallid form of Mr. John by the hair of his head, whose livid lips uttered the awful words, "Justo judicio Dei judicatus sum; justo judicio Dei condemnatus sum"—"I am judged and condemned by the just judgment of God." I was horror-struck; and instantly throwing the jingling purse into the abyss, I exclaimed, "Wretch! in the name of Heaven, I conjure you to be gone!—away from my sight!—never appear before me again!" With a dark expression on his countenance, he arose, and immediately vanished behind the huge rocks which surrounded the place.

Chapter V

I was now left equally without gold and without shadow; but a heavy load was taken from my breast, and I felt cheerful. Had not my Minna been irrecoverably lost to me, or even had I been perfectly free from self-reproach on her account, I felt that happiness might yet have been mine. At present I was lost in doubt as to my future course. I examined my pockets, and found I had a few gold pieces still left, which I counted with feelings of great satisfaction. I had left my horse at the inn, and was ashamed to return, or at all events I must wait till the sun had set, which at present was high in the heavens. I laid myself down under a shady tree and fell into a peaceful sleep.

Lovely forms floated in airy measures before me, and filled up my delightful dreams. Minna, with a garland of flowers entwined in her hair, was bending over me with a smile of goodwill; also the worthy Bendel was crowned with flowers, and hastened to meet me with friendly greetings. Many other forms seemed to rise up confusedly in the distance: thyself among the number, Chamisso. Perfect radiance beamed around them, but none had a shadow; and what was more surprising, there was no appearance of unhappiness on this account. Nothing was to be seen or heard but flowers and music; and love and joy, and groves of never-fading palms, seemed the natives of that happy clime.

In vain I tried to detain and comprehend the lovely but fleeting forms. I was conscious, also, of being in a dream, and was anxious that nothing should rouse me from it; and when I did awake, I kept my eyes closed, in order if possible to continue the illusion. At last I opened my eyes. The sun was now visible in the east; I must have slept the whole night: I looked upon this as a warning not to return to the inn. What I had left there I was content to lose, without much regret; and resigning myself to Providence, I decided on taking a by-road that led through the wooded declivity of the mountain. I never once cast a glance behind me; nor did it ever occur to me to return, as I might have done, to Bendel, whom I had left in affluence. I reflected on the new character I was now going to assume in the world. My present garb was very humble—consisting of an old black coat I formerly had worn at Berlin, and which by some chance was the first I put my hand on before setting out on this journey, a travelling-cap, and an old pair of boots. I cut down a knotted stick in memory of the spot, and commenced my pilgrimage.

In the forest I met an aged peasant, who gave me a friendly greeting, and with whom I entered into conversation, requesting, as a traveller desirous of information, some particulars relative to the road, the country, and its inhabitants, the productions of the mountain, &c. He replied to my various inquiries with readiness and intelligence. At last we reached the bed of a mountain-torrent, which had laid waste a considerable tract of the forest; I inwardly shuddered at the idea of the open sunshine. I suffered the peasant to go before me. In the middle of the very place which I dreaded so much, he suddenly stopped, and turned back to give me an account of this inundation; but instantly perceiving that I had no shadow, he broke off abruptly, and exclaimed, "How is this?—you have no shadow!"

"Alas, alas!" said I, "in a long and serious illness I had the misfortune to lose my hair, my nails, and my shadow. Look, good father; although my hair has grown again, it is quite white; and at my age, my nails are still very short; and my poor shadow seems to have left me, never to return."

"Ah!" said the old man, shaking his head; "no shadow! that was indeed a terrible illness, sir."

But he did not resume his narrative; and at the very first cross-road we came to, left me without uttering a syllable. Fresh tears flowed from my eyes, and my cheerfulness had fled. With a heavy heart I travelled on, avoiding all society. I plunged into the deepest shades of the forest; and often, to avoid a sunny tract of country, I waited for hours till every human being had left it, and I could pass it unobserved. In the evenings I took shelter in the villages. I bent my steps to a mine in the mountains, where I hoped to meet with work underground; for besides that my present situation compelled me to provide for my own support, I felt that incessant and laborious occupation alone could divert my mind from dwelling on painful subjects. A few rainy days assisted me materially on my journey; but it was to the no small detriment of my boots, the soles of which were better suited to Count Peter than to the poor foot-traveller. I was soon barefoot, and a new purchase must be made. The following morning I commenced an earnest search in a market-place, where a fair was being held; and I saw in one of the booths new and second-hand boots set out for sale. I was a long time selecting and bargaining; I wished much to have a new pair, but was frightened at the extravagant price; and so was obliged to content myself with a second-hand pair, still pretty good and strong, which the beautiful fair-haired youth who kept the booth handed over to me with a cheerful smile, wishing me a prosperous journey. I went on, and left the place immediately by the northern gate.

I was so lost in my own thoughts, that I walked along scarcely knowing how or where. I was calculating the chances of my reaching the mine by the evening, and considering how I should introduce myself. I had not gone two hundred steps, when I perceived I was not in the right road. I looked round, and found myself in a wild-looking forest of ancient firs, where apparently the stroke of the axe had never been heard. A few steps more brought me amid huge rocks covered with moss and saxifragous plants, between which whole fields of snow and ice were extended. The air was intensely cold. I looked round, and the forest had disappeared behind me; a few steps more, and there was the stillness of death itself. The icy plain on which I stood stretched to an immeasurable distance, and a thick cloud rested upon it; the sun was of a red blood-colour at the verge of the horizon; the cold was insupportable. I could not imagine what had happened to me. The benumbing frost made me quicken my pace. I heard a distant sound of waters; and, at one step more, I stood on the icy shore of some ocean. Innumerable droves of sea-dogs rushed past me and plunged into the waves. I continued my way along this coast, and again met with rocks, plains, birch and fir forests, and yet only a few minutes had elapsed. It was now intensely hot. I looked around, and suddenly found myself between some fertile rice-fields and mulberry-trees; I sat down under their shade, and found by my watch that it was just one quarter of an hour since I had left the village market. I fancied it was a dream; but no, I was indeed awake, as I felt by the experiment I made of biting my tongue. I closed my eyes in order to collect my scattered thoughts. Presently I heard unintelligible words uttered in a nasal tone; and I beheld two Chinese, whose Asiatic physiognomies were not to be mistaken, even had their costume not betrayed their origin. They were addressing me in the language and with the salutations of their country. I rose, and drew back a couple of steps. They had disappeared; the landscape was entirely changed; the rice-fields had given place to trees and woods. I examined some of the trees and plants around me, and ascertained such of them as I was acquainted with to be productions of the southern part of Asia. I made one step towards a particular tree, and again all was changed. I now moved on like a recruit at drill, taking slow and measured steps, gazing with astonished eyes at the wonderful variety of regions, plains, meadows, mountains, steppes, and sandy deserts, which passed in succession before me. I had now no doubt that I had seven-leagued boots on my feet.

I fell on my knees in silent gratitude, shedding tears of thankfulness; for I now saw clearly what was to be my future condition. Shut out by early sins from all human society, I was offered amends for the privation by Nature herself, which I had ever loved. The earth was granted me as a rich garden; and the knowledge of her operations was to be the study and object of my life. This was not a mere resolution. I have since endeavoured, with anxious and unabated industry, faithfully to imitate the finished and brilliant model then presented to me; and my vanity has received a check when led to compare the picture with the original. I rose immediately, and took a hasty survey of this new field, where I hoped afterwards to reap a rich harvest.

I stood on the heights of Thibet; and the sun I had lately beheld in the east was now sinking in the west. I traversed Asia from east to west, and thence passed into Africa, which I curiously examined at repeated visits in all directions. As I gazed on the ancient pyramids and temples of Egypt, I descried, in the sandy deserts near Thebes of the hundred gates, the caves where Christian hermits dwelt of old. My determination was instantly taken, that here should be my future dwelling. I chose one of the most secluded, but roomy, comfortable, and inaccessible to the jackals.

I stepped over from the pillars of Hercules to Europe; and having taken a survey of its northern and southern countries, I passed by the north of Asia, on the polar glaciers, to Greenland and America, visiting both parts of this continent; and the winter, which was already at its height in the south, drove me quickly back from Cape Horn to the north. I waited till daylight had risen in the east of Asia, and then, after a short rest, continued my pilgrimage. I followed in both the Americas the vast chain of the Andes, once considered the loftiest on our globe. I stepped carefully and slowly from one summit to another, sometimes over snowy heights, sometimes over flaming volcanoes, often breathless from fatigue. At last I reached Elias's mountain, and sprang over Behring's Straits into Asia; I followed the western coast in its various windings, carefully observing which of the neighbouring isles was accessible to me. From the peninsula of Malacca, my boots carried me to Sumatra, Java, Bali, and Lombok. I made many attempts—often with danger, and always unsuccessfully—to force my way over the numerous little islands and rocks with which this sea is studded, wishing to find a north-west passage to Borneo and other islands of the Archipelago.

At last I sat down at the extreme point of Lombok, my eyes turned towards the south-east, lamenting that I had so soon reached the limits allotted to me, and bewailing my fate as a captive in his grated cell. Thus was I shut out from that remarkable country, New Holland, and the islands of the southern ocean, so essentially necessary to a knowledge of the earth, and which would have best assisted me in the study of the animal and vegetable kingdoms. And thus, at the very outset, I beheld all my labours condemned to be limited to mere fragments.

Ah! Chamisso, what is the activity of man?

Frequently in the most rigorous winters of the southern hemisphere I have rashly thrown myself on a fragment of drifting ice between Cape Horn and Van Dieman's Land, in the hope of effecting a passage to New Holland, reckless of the cold and the vast ocean, reckless of my fate, even should this savage land prove my grave.

But all in vain—I never reached New Holland. Each time, when defeated in my attempt, I returned to Lombok; and seated at its extreme point, my eyes directed to the south-east, I gave way afresh to lamentations that my range of investigation was so limited. At last I tore myself from the spot, and, heartily grieved at my disappointment, returned to the interior of Asia. Setting out at morning dawn, I traversed it from east to west, and at night reached the cave in Thebes which I had previously selected for my dwelling-place, and had visited yesterday afternoon.

After a short repose, as soon as daylight had visited Europe, it was my first care to provide myself with the articles of which I stood most in need. First of all a drag, to act on my boots; for I had experienced the inconvenience of these whenever I wished to shorten my steps and examine surrounding objects more fully. A pair of slippers to go over the boots served the purpose effectually; and from that time I carried two pairs about me, because I frequently cast them off from my feet in my botanical investigations, without having time to pick them up, when threatened by the approach of lions, men, or hyenas. My excellent watch, owing to the short duration of my movements, was also on these occasions an admirable chronometer. I wanted, besides, a sextant, a few philosophical instruments, and some books. To purchase these things, I made several unwilling journeys to London and Paris, choosing a time when I could be hid by the favouring clouds. As all my ill-gotten gold was exhausted, I carried over from Africa some ivory, which is there so plentiful, in payment of my purchases—taking care, however, to pick out the smallest teeth, in order not to over-burden myself. I had thus soon provided myself with all that I wanted, and now entered on a new mode of life as a student—wandering over the globe—measuring the height of the mountains, and the temperature of the air and of the springs—observing the manners and habits of animals—investigating plants and flowers. From the equator to the pole, and from the new world to the old, I was constantly engaged in repeating and comparing my experiments. My usual food consisted of the eggs of the African ostrich or northern sea-birds, with a few fruits, especially those of the palm and the banana of the tropics. The tobacco-plant consoled me when I was depressed; and the affection of my spaniel was a compensation for the loss of human sympathy and society. When I returned from my excursions, loaded with fresh treasures, to my cave in Thebes, which he guarded during my absence, he ever sprang joyfully forward to greet me, and made me feel that I was indeed not alone on the earth. An adventure soon occurred which brought me once more among my fellow-creatures.

One day, as I was gathering lichens and algae on the northern coast, with the drag on my boots, a bear suddenly made his appearance, and was stealing towards me round the corner of a rock. After throwing away my slippers, I attempted to step across to an island, by means of a rock, projecting from the waves in the intermediate space, that served as a stepping-stone. I reached the rock safely with one foot, but instantly fell into the sea with the other, one of my slippers having inadvertently remained on. The cold was intense; and I escaped this imminent peril at the risk of my life. On coming ashore, I hastened to the Libyan sands to dry myself in the sun; but the heat affected my head so much, that, in a fit of illness, I staggered back to the north. In vain I sought relief by change of place—hurrying from east to west, and from west to east—now in climes of the south, now in those of the north; sometimes I rushed into daylight, sometimes into the shades of night. I know not how long this lasted. A burning fever raged in my veins; with extreme anguish I felt my senses leaving me. Suddenly, by an unlucky accident, I trod upon some one's foot, whom I had hurt, and received a blow in return which laid me senseless.

On recovering, I found myself lying comfortably in a good bed, which, with many other beds, stood in a spacious and handsome apartment. Some one was watching by me; people seemed to be walking from one bed to another; they came beside me, and spoke of me as *number twelve*. On the wall, at the foot of my bed—it was no dream, for I distinctly read it—on a black-marble tablet was inscribed my name, in large letters of gold:

PETER SCHLEMIHL

Underneath were two rows of letters in smaller characters, which I was too feeble to connect together, and closed my eyes again.

I now heard something read aloud, in which I distinctly noted the words, "Peter Schlemihl," but could not collect the full meaning. I saw a man of benevolent aspect, and a very beautiful female dressed in black, standing near my bed; their countenances were not unknown to me, but in my weak state I could not remember who they were. Some time elapsed, and I began to regain my strength. I was called Number Twelve, and, from my long beard, was supposed to be a Jew, but was not the less carefully nursed on that account. No one seemed to perceive that I was destitute of a shadow. My boots, I was assured, together with everything found on me when I was brought here, were in safe keeping, and would be given up to me on my restoration to health. This place was called the *Schlemihlium*: the daily recitation I had heard, was an exhortation to pray for Peter Schlemihl as the founder and benefactor of this institution. The benevolent-looking man whom I had seen by my bedside was Bendel; the beautiful lady in black was Minna.

I had been enjoying the advantages of the Schlemihlium without being recognised; and I learned, further, that I was in Bendel's native town, where he had employed a part of my once unhallowed gold in founding an hospital in my name, under his superintendence, and that its unfortunate inmates daily pronounced blessings on me. Minna had become a widow: an unhappy lawsuit had deprived Rascal of his life, and Minna of the greater part of her property. Her parents were no more; and here she dwelt in widowed piety, wholly devoting herself to works of mercy.

One day, as she stood by the side of Number Twelve's bed with Bendel, he said to her, "Noble lady, why expose yourself so frequently to this unhealthy atmosphere? Has fate dealt so harshly with you as to render you desirous of death?"

"By no means, Mr. Bendel," she replied; "since I have awoke from my long dream, all has gone well with me. I now neither wish for death nor fear it, and think on the future and on the past with equal serenity. Do you not also feel an inward satisfaction in thus paying a pious tribute of gratitude and love to your old master and friend?"

"Thanks be to God, I do, noble lady," said he. "Ah, how wonderfully has everything fallen out! How thoughtlessly have we sipped joys and sorrows from the full cup now drained to the last drop; and we might fancy the past a mere prelude to the real scene for which we now wait armed by experience. How different has been the reality! Yet let us not regret the past, but rather rejoice that we have not lived in vain. As respects our old friend also, I have a firm hope that it is now better with him than formerly."

"I trust so, too," answered Minna; and so saying she passed by me, and they departed.

This conversation made a deep impression on me; and I hesitated whether I should discover myself or depart unknown. At last I decided; and, asking for pen and paper, wrote as follows:—

"Matters are indeed better with your old friend than formerly. He has repented; and his repentance has led to forgiveness."

I now attempted to rise, for I felt myself stronger. The keys of a little chest near my bed were given me; and in it I found all my effects. I put on my clothes; fastened my botanical case round me—wherein, with delight, I found my northern lichens all safe—put on my boots, and leaving my note on the table, left the gates, and was speedily far advanced on the road to Thebes.

Passing along the Syrian coast, which was the same road I had taken on last leaving home, I beheld my poor Figaro running to meet me. The faithful animal, after vainly waiting at home for his master's return, had probably followed his traces. I stood still, and called him. He sprang towards me with leaps and barks, and a thousand demonstrations of unaffected delight. I took him in my arms—for he was unable to follow me—and carried him home.

There I found everything exactly in the order in which I had left it; and returned by degrees, as my increasing strength allowed me, to my old occupations and usual mode of life, from which I was kept back a whole year by my fall into the Polar Ocean. And this, dear Chamisso, is the life I am still leading. My boots are not yet worn out, as I had been led to fear would be the case from that very learned work of Tieckius—De rebus gestis Pollicilli. Their energies remain unimpaired; and although mine are gradually failing me, I enjoy the consolation of having spent them in pursuing incessantly one object, and that not fruitlessly.

So far as my boots would carry me, I have observed and studied our globe and its conformation, its mountains and temperature, the atmosphere in its various changes, the influences of the magnetic power; in fact, I have studied all living creation—and more especially the kingdom of plants—more profoundly than any one of our race. I have arranged all the facts in proper order, to the best of my ability, in different works. The consequences deducible from these facts, and my views respecting them, I have hastily recorded in some essays and dissertations. I have settled the geography of the interior of Africa and the Arctic regions, of the interior of Asia and of its eastern coast. My Historia stirpium plantarum utriusque orbis is an extensive fragment of a Flora universalis terrae and a part of my Systema naturae. Besides increasing the number of our known species by more than a third, I have also contributed somewhat to the natural system of plants and to a knowledge of their geography. I am now deeply engaged on my Fauna, and shall take care to have my manuscripts sent to the University of Berlin before my decease.

I have selected thee, my dear Chamisso, to be the guardian of my wonderful history, thinking that, when I have left this world, it may afford valuable instruction to the living.

As for thee, Chamisso, if thou wouldst live amongst thy fellow-creatures, learn to value thy shadow more than gold; if thou wouldst only live to thyself and thy nobler part—in this thou needest no counsel.

Adalbert Stifter

Across the Steppes

There are often incidents and relationships in life whose meaning is not immediately clear to us and whose background is not readily understandable. And then, just because they are rather mysterious, they exercise a certain gentle and quite pleasant attraction on us. The features of a quite plain person often impress us as having a real inner beauty, though we are not always immediately able to say why. On the other hand, we often find a face cold and empty though all others assure us that its features are of great beauty. In the same way we will occasionally find ourselves quite strongly attracted to someone we really hardly know at all. We like his bearing perhaps, or we find his personality engaging. We are sorry when the acquaintance ends, and in later years when we call him to mind we experience a feeling almost of sadness, a kind of longing, even something approaching affection. On the other hand, we sometimes find that a person whose worth is attested by many things nevertheless means little to us even after we have been acquainted with him for years.

There is no doubt that in such cases there are intangible factors at work, things that affect the heart, and we are not able to analyse the matter deliberately and arrive at logical conclusions. Psychology has now explained a great many things to us, but others remain unfathomable and still beyond our reach. It is hardly too much to say that even in our world there is a certain immeasurable and serene zone in which God and the intangible are at work still. In moments of rapture the soul will sometimes cross its borders impetuously, and in childlike artlessness poetry too will occasionally raise the veil. But stark science with its cautious calculations can never venture farther than the edge, and usually it is quite content to have neither hand nor part in such mysteries.

Such thoughts were aroused in my mind by an experience that once fell to my lot as a very young man on the estate of an old Major, a very good friend of mine. It happened at a time when the restlessness of youth was still sending me here, there and everywhere in the hope of experiencing or discovering God alone knows exactly what.

I had got to know this Major whilst I was in Italy and on several occasions he invited me to visit him in his own country. However, at the time I regarded the invitation as more or less a polite formality, the sort of amiability travellers do often exchange at their casual meetings, and I should probably have thought no more about the matter, but some long time afterwards I received a friendly letter from him inquiring after my welfare and concluding by repeating once again his old invitation and suggesting that I should stay with him on his estate in Hungary for a summer, or for longer if I had a mind—for a year or for five years, since he had at last made up his mind to stay in one place, in one very small spot on this earth, and to let no other dust settle on his feet henceforth but that of his own country, where he had, so he declared, at last found an aim in life that he had sought in vain elsewhere throughout the world.

It was spring when I received this letter and as I was curious to know just what was the aim to which he referred, and as, also, I was at a loss at that moment to know where to go next, I decided to do as he suggested and so I accepted his invitation.

His estate was in Eastern Hungary and for a couple of days I occupied myself with various plans for making my journey as comfortable and convenient as possible. The third day saw me in a mail coach rolling eastward, my mind greatly occupied with thoughts of heaths and woodlands, for

I had never visited his country before. On the eighth day I was already crossing the famous pusta, a barren, level heath probably as magnificent and as lonely as any Hungary had to offer.

At first I was completely under the spell of its immense endlessness. A fresh breeze ceaselessly caressed my face, the smell of the steppes was constantly in my nostrils, and a uniform loneliness stretched away in all directions. And so it remained the next day and the day after that, and the day after that again, always the same far-away horizon where heaven and earth met. I therefore soon became accustomed to it and my eye grew less curious. Surfeited by the immense, unchanging emptiness my mind withdrew into itself and as the sun shone on persistently and the grass glistened endlessly in its rays, other thoughts arose. Older memories crowded in as I rolled across the heath, and, in particular, my recollections of the man to whom I was now making my way. I welcomed the memories and in that lonely expanse of heath around me I had time enough and inclination to recall all I had ever known about him and to reconstruct the former picture in my mind.

I had first met him in Southern Italy, in a barren waste almost as austere as the one through which I was now passing. In those days he had been an honoured and welcome guest everywhere, and although even then he was almost fifty years of age, more than one pair of beautiful eyes had been drawn to him, for never was there a man whose build and whose features more deserved the description of handsome, or a man who bore himself with greater nobility. In addition there was a certain gentle modesty in his bearing which was so natural and so engaging that men too were won by it. And as for women, it was rumoured—and I can well believe it—that in younger years his effect on them had been devastating. There were many stories current concerning his conquests and many of them were remarkable. But, they said, there was one thing lacking in him: the ability to respond truly, and it was this that made him really dangerous. No one, not even the greatest beauty, had ever succeeded in holding him for long. To the very end he would behave

himself with all the charm that won him every heart and
filled the lady of the moment with enraptured triumph, but
then, when he was so minded, he would make his farewell,
set out on his travels once more—and never return. But, far
from discouraging women, this behaviour seemed to attract
them still more, and more than one hot-blooded woman of
southern climes could hardly control her impatience or wait
to offer him both heart and devotion. And the fact that no
one knew from whence he came or what was his position in
the world was nothing but an added ground for attraction.

But although the Graces had clearly chosen him for their
own, there was yet an indication of some sorrow on his
brow, a sign that in the past at least his emotions had perhaps not lacked profundity. And it was just that past that
puzzled and interested people so greatly, and that above all
because no one had the slightest inkling of what had been
his past. There were rumours, of course: he had been em-
broiled in matters of State; he had been unhappily married;
he had shot his own brother... And other suggestions of a
like dramatic nature. However, the only certain thing people did know was not about his past: it was that now he was
keenly interested in the progress of science.

I had already heard a great deal about him before I first
met him, tossing stones into the crater of Vesuvius and
watching the blue smoke that wreathed up from time to
time from the main crater and from various fissures. I recognized him at once from the descriptions I had heard and I
went towards him between the yellow boulders which were
strewn around. He answered amiably when I spoke to him
and soon we were talking animatedly. The scene around us
at the time was truly desolate, a gloomy waste, and the effect was heightened by the indescribably lovely blue of the
Southern Italian sky above us into which slow billows of
smoke rose sadly and erratically from the crater. We chatted
for some time in a very friendly fashion but when we finally
parted each went his separate way down the mountain-side.

Later on opportunity arose for us to meet again and after
that we exchanged a number of visits and by the time I had

decided to return home we were very close friends, almost inseparable. I found that he was more or less unconscious of the effect his personality and appearance produced on those around him. Although he was then approaching fifty years of age, there was a certain youthful impetuousness in him which broke out from time to time as though even in the middle years his life and his character were far from settled. And as I became more closely acquainted with him I discovered that his nature was more generous, more that of a poet, than that of any man I had as yet encountered. Because of this there was often something childlike, something even ingenuous, about him. He was clearly quite unaware of these things and in all naturalness his language was more beautiful than any I have ever heard on human lips. Throughout my life—even later on when I associated a great deal with artists and poets—I never encountered such a sensitive feeling for beauty, though it could certainly be provoked to impatience by grossness. It was probably these gifts, of which he seemed unconscious, that won him the hearts of all women, for such brilliance is unusual in men of middle years. Now although I was a very young man at the time and really not in a position to appreciate such qualities at their true worth, he seemed to be very willingly in my company. It was, in fact, not until I grew older—and in particular when I began to set down the story of his life—that I came to understand and appreciate such things.

What truth there was in the fabulous stories of his successes with women I never discovered, because he never spoke about such things himself and I never had any personal opportunity for judging. I was also never able to discover anything about the reason for that sadness that seemed on him. All I could find out about his earlier life was that as a young man he had been always on the move. In recent years, however, he seemed more or less to have settled down in Naples, where he devoted himself to the study of volcanic lava and antiquities. It was from his own lips that I learned that he had lands in Hungary, and, as I have already said, he repeatedly invited me to come and visit him there.

We were close friends for quite a long time and when I finally went away it was not without emotion that we separated. Subsequently my mind was so occupied with many different countries and many different people that it never even occurred to me as a possibility that I should one day be travelling across the Hungarian pusta to visit him, as I was now in fact doing. With so much time to spare on my journey my mind turned more and more to my recollections of him and I reconstructed the old picture so successfully in my memory that now and again I had some difficulty in realizing that I was not once again in Italy, particularly as the steppe landscape through which I was passing was as hot and silent as Italy had been, and at the same time the bluish haze in the distance mirrored itself in my eye as an optical illusion of the Pontine Marshes.

I did not make straight for the Major's estate, whose whereabouts he had described to me in detail in his letters. Instead I travelled here and there through the country-side, wishing to take advantage of the opportunity to get thoroughly acquainted with it. Because of what my friend had told me so often about it, the picture in my mind had merged more and more with what I knew about Italy, but now it began to develop its own individuality and to become an independent entity for me. Since setting out I had crossed scores of rivulets, streams and rivers and I had often shared the humble shelter of the herdsmen of the plains and their shaggy dogs. I had drunk from those steppe wells with their typical high poles jutting up into the sky at a sharp angle and I had slept under more than one of those low-eaved thatched roofs that characterized the countryside. Here the bagpipe player would take his ease, there the busy carter would drive his horses rapidly over the heath, whilst in the distance glistened the white coat of the horse-minder.

I often wondered whether I should find my friend at all changed in such surroundings. I had previously seen him only in society, in company where one man looks very much like another. There he had been the polished gentleman moving amongst his kind. But here everything was so different, and often, when for whole days I saw nothing but the reddish-blue shimmer of the rolling steppes relieved only by innumerable white specks where the cattle grazed, I wondered how he would fit into it all. The soil beneath my feet was dark and rich, giving rise to a wild and luxuriant growth, and despite the country's ancient history there was something new and elemental about it all. As I travelled around in this countryside and learned to know its character and its individuality it sometimes seemed to me that I could hear the ringing blows of the hammer that was falling on the anvil as the future of this people was forged. Those things that have had their day and are passing away are tired and weary, but those things that are still becoming are fiery and vigorous. This, it seemed to me, was a country of the future and I found myself taking a keen pleasure in its innumerable villages, its fine vineyards stretching up the hillsides, its broad marshes with their luxuriant reeds, and, far in the distance, the soft blue mountains that framed it all.

After months of wandering around in this fashion I realized one day that I must be somewhere quite close to my friend's estate, and, a little tired now of my travels, I decided to make straight for where I was long expected. That afternoon I had trudged through an arid waste of stones. Far away to the left the blue summits of mountains rose into the sky. They were the Carpathians, I judged. To the right was broken countryside with the peculiar reddish coloration of the steppes. Between the two was the seemingly endless sweep of the plains. After crossing the bed of a dried-out stream I climbed slowly out of a small valley and to the right I saw a wood of chestnut trees and a white house.

Three miles. Three miles. That was what I had been told all the afternoon when I asked the way to Unwar, which was the name of the Major's house and estate. Three miles. But by this time I had learned what a Hungarian mile was. I had certainly gone at least five ordinary miles already and I therefore hoped devoutly that the white house I could now see—previously I had been unsighted by a sand drift— would prove to be Unwar. In the middle distance tilled fields rose up to a sort of causeway on which I could see figures. I decided to ask if the white house were, in fact, Unwar, and to reach the men I could see there I cut through the verge of the chestnut wood.

Before long I observed what I had already guessed from my previous experience of the deceptive lie of this country-side: that the house was not really by the wood at all but at the other side of a level stretch of land that ran away from it. It became clear too that it must be a very large house. At that moment I saw a rider galloping across the level stretch of land towards the fields where the men were working. When this rider came up with them the men gathered round him as though he were their master. At that I looked keenly at the horseman but the figure looked nothing like that of my friend the Major. Without hurrying I made my way towards the causeway, which was farther away than I had at first thought, and as I came up with the group the rays of the sinking sun were turning red as they fell across the rich maize fields and on the group of bearded men as they stood around the rid-er. To my surprise this rider turned out to be a woman. She was perhaps forty years of age and she was wearing the wide trousers of the countryside and sitting astride her horse like a man. By the time I reached her the labourers were already go-ing back to their work and she was almost alone. I therefore directed my inquiries to her. Resting my pack on my stick and raising one hand to protect my eyes from the still strong rays of the sun I looked up at her and spoke in German.

'Good evening, ma'am.'

'Good evening,' she replied in the same language.

'Would you be so good as to tell me whether that white house over yonder is Unwar ?'

'No. That isn't Unwar. Is it Unwar you want ?'

'Yes. An old friend of mine lives there, a Major. He has invited me to visit him.'

'Oh, yes. Very well, follow me. I will set you on your way to Unwar.'

She moved off slowly on her horse so that I could keep up with her, making her way still farther up the slope between the high ears of maize. As I followed behind her I had ample opportunity to look around at the countryside and what I saw astonished me more and more. The higher we went up the hill the more the valley opened up behind us and I saw that the wood beyond the white house was very large and stretched away to the mountains. Great avenues of trees came right down to the fields and one cultivated area after the other was revealed with crops which all seemed in excellent heart. I had never seen such long, plump and healthy-looking maize before and it was obviously most carefully tended, for there was no grass or weeds growing between its strong stems. The vineyard whose edge we were now approaching reminded me of the Rhineland, but I had never seen quite such rich foliage or such luscious berries; they seemed almost bursting with juice. The level ground between the chestnut trees and the house was meadowland and it looked as soft and green as though it were a stretch of fine satin. The ways across this meadowland were all fenced in neatly and between them white cattle, as smooth and shapely as deer, grazed peacefully. This rich landscape was in striking contrast to the stony waste I had previously trudged through. It lay behind me now, looking dry and parched in the red rays of the sun by comparison with the cool, green freshness of this richly cultivated soil.

In a little while we arrived at one of the small white huts I had noticed dotted around here and there against the darker green of the vineyards and the woman spoke to a young fellow who was working there. Despite the warmth of the July evening he was wearing a shaggy fur coat.

'Milosch, this gentleman wishes to get to Unwar today. Take a couple of the horses and go with him as far as the gallows.'

'Yes, Ma'am,' said the young fellow obediently, abandoning what he was doing.

'Go with him now,' said the woman to me. 'He will put you safely on your way.'

And with that she turned her horse's head and was about to ride away. I took her to be some sort of estate overseer and I wanted to give her something in return for the service she had done me, but she smiled and shook her head and I noticed that she had very beautiful white teeth. She rode her horse slowly down the vineyard slope but soon afterwards I heard the rapid beat of hooves as she galloped away across the flat ground below.

I put my money away and turned to the young fellow she had addressed as Milosch. He now put on a broad-brimmed hat in addition to his fur coat and then he led me through the vineyard. After a while the ground sloped down again and we came to some farm buildings. Going to the stables he led out two of the small wiry horses of which there are so many in this part of the world. One he saddled for me but the other he mounted bare back and together we set off in the deepening twilight towards the darkening eastern horizon. We must have presented an odd picture as we rode along together: the German wanderer with his pack, his knotted stick and his cap, and the slim young Hungarian with his long, drooping moustaches, his round, broad-brimmed hat, his fur coat and his wide, flapping trousers.

On the other side of the vineyards was wasteland and the prosperous settlement lay behind us now like a vanished fairy land. This wasteland was actually part of the stony waste I had tramped through earlier that day and it was so much the same to the eye that I could have thought we were going back the way I had come but for the fact that the dying red across the horizon behind me told me that we really were going eastward.

'How far is Unwar?' I asked.

'About another mile and a half,' the young fellow answered. I kept up with him as well as I could and we passed the same innumerable grey boulders I had already seen by the thousand that day. They now glimmered with a false light against the dark ground and we rode between them on firm moorland, the hooves of our horses making no sound except when occasionally their shoes rang out against a stone. Our beasts were obviously used to such going, however, and they usually managed to pick their way safely between the stones. The way was level on the whole but now and again there were small depressions. We rode down one side and up the other and at the bottom of each of these small valleys there was a petrified stream of scree.

'Who owns the estate we have just left?' I asked.

'Maroshely,' he answered.

He spoke without reining in and I was not certain whether that was the name of the owner or the estate, or whether I had even caught it correctly. The movement of our horses made it difficult to speak or to hear what was spoken.

An orange moon had now begun to rise and in its first faint light I distinguished a tall scaffolding looming up on the heath ahead of us. I took it to be the gallows to which my companion had been instructed to lead me, and so it was.

'This is the gallows,' he said almost immediately, and he reined in his horse. 'Down below there is a stream. Look, you can see it glistening. That black mass near it is an oak tree. That's where they used to hang wrongdoers at one time. It isn't used now that we've got a real gallows up here. On the other side of that oak tree you'll find a path.

There are young trees on either side. Go along that for about an hour and you'll come to a gate in a fence. You'll see a bell pull there. Ring the bell, but don't go in even if the gate's unlocked—because of the dogs. Dismount now. And do up your jacket or you might catch fever.'

I dismounted and although I had not had much luck with the supposed overseer I offered Milosch some money. He accepted it without question and tucked it away somewhere inside his fur jacket, murmuring a word of thanks. Then he took the reins of my horse, turned the two horses about and galloped off at once even before I had time to ask him to thank the owner of the horses for his kindness in allowing me, a complete stranger, to ride off on one of them at such a late hour. Milosch seemed anxious to get away from the neighbourhood of the gallows as quickly as possible. In the yellow moonlight I could see that it consisted of nothing but two upright poles and a cross beam. I rather fancied that there was something hanging from it, but that could have been imagination and I made no attempt to find out. Nothing loath I quickly left it behind me too and went off at a good pace through the long grass, which had seemed almost to be whispering as it caressed the foot of the gallows.

There was now neither sight nor sound of Milosch and there might never have been such a person. I quickly came to the stream, which glistened and rippled through the rushes like a snake. Above it loomed the black mass of the old oak that had once been a gallows tree and on the other side I found that path Milosch had described. It was of beaten earth with a ditch on either side and it looked almost white in the moon between long lines of young poplars. My steps as they sounded on this harder ground were vaguely comforting; it was almost as though I were walking along one of the familiar paths at home.

I went forward steadily and the moon rose higher and brighter until finally it rode at full strength in the warm summer sky shining down on the heath that stretched away on either side, grey and robbed of all its normal colour. I had walked for about an hour when black clumps of trees rose up ahead as though I were coming to the beginning of a wood. Soon after that I came to a gate set in a high fence that ran out of the trees. Behind it the massive crowns of many great trees stood out still and silent in the silver light of the moon. There was a bell pull at the gate, as Milosch had said, and I gave it a good tug. A bell rang somewhere at a distance and then, instead of barking, I heard a deep, snorting, snuffling sound such as big dogs make, followed immediately by a thud as the beast sprang at the gate. It was one of the most magnificent dogs I have ever seen and it stood on its hind legs with its fore paws against the bars of the gate, staring at me without making a sound as such great solemn beasts will.

After a moment or two it was joined by two younger and smaller dogs of the same breed which ran up prancing and growling. They were fine mastiff dogs and all three now stood there together and stared at me unwinkingly. After a while I heard footsteps and a man came up to the gate wearing the inevitable shaggy fur coat. In answer to his question as to my business I asked if this were Unwar and I mentioned my name. He obviously already had his instructions and at the mention of my name he immediately called off the dogs with a few sharp words in Hungarian and opened the gate.

'The master has received your letters, sir,' he said as he closed the gate behind me and led me along the path. 'He has been expecting you for some time.'

'I told him in my last letter that I wanted to see something of the countryside first,' I replied.

'I hope you have enjoyed it, sir,' he said.

'Yes, I did. Is the Major still up ?'

'He isn't at home at all today, sir. He's at the session. Tomorrow morning he'll ride back. But rooms are prepared for you and we have instructions to make you as comfortable as possible should you arrive in his absence.'

'Very well—if you'd be good enough to do that.'

'Most certainly, sir.'

This was the only conversation that took place between us during the rather long walk through the park. It put me in mind of a well-kept jungle. Enormous fir trees reared into the sky and limbs of oak as thick as a man's middle stretched out all around. The biggest dog trotted quietly along at our side, but the other two, not yet so well behaved, sniffed at my clothing from time to time and danced around us. When we had gone through the park we came to a treeless rise on which the Major's house stood. As far as I could see in the light of the moon that fell lambently upon it, it was a large four-cornered building. A flight of broad stone steps led up to a terrace and the house was surrounded by railings. The man led me to a gate in these railings and then he said a word or two to the dogs, which immediately turned about and trotted back into the park. Opening the gate the man then led me into the house.

Lights were burning on the staircase and they shone on a row of strange statues representing men in wide-topped high boots and flowing garments. They might have been former Hungarian kings. On the first floor we entered a long corridor laid out with rush matting. At the end of this corridor we went up another flight of steps and came into another such corridor. Opening a wing of one of the doors along this corridor my guide invited me to enter and informed me that these were to be my quarters. He followed me inside and after he had lit a great many more candles in each of the three rooms of which my quarters consisted he wished me good night and went away. Shortly after that another manservant brought me wine, bread and cold roast meat. He too then bowed, bade me good night and departed. As I was obviously to be left to my own devices now I went to the doors and closed them.

After that I sat down and made a good supper and then I looked at my leisure around my new quarters. The first room, in which my meal had been laid out at one end of a long table, was very large, almost a small hall, but so many candles were burning that it was very well lit. It was furnished rather differently from the fashion I was accustomed to at home. Down the centre was the long table at which I had eaten and along its sides were oaken benches. There were only one or two ordinary chairs and the general impression was formal rather than comfortable—as though the place were really intended for meetings. On the walls hung ancient weapons from various historical periods. They were probably mostly Hungarian and there were many bows and arrows. Apart from these weapons there were also costumes displayed on the walls as though in a museum. They seemed chiefly to be Hungarian costumes of other days but here and there were also silken garments that had probably been worn at one time by Turks, or perhaps Tartars.

Giving off this main chamber there were two other rooms that had been placed at my disposal and when I went into them I noticed with approval that they were rather more comfortably furnished. There were chairs, tables, wardrobes, writing accommodation and materials and washing arrangements—in fact there was everything to make a traveller feel at his ease after a long and tiring journey. There were even books on a bedside table and I noticed that they were all in German. In each of these two smaller rooms there was a bed. One of them was draped with the wide Hungarian garment known as a 'Bunda' instead of the ordinary covering. This Bunda is usually a mantle of furs worn with the rough side inwards, and the smooth outer skins are often decorated with gaily coloured straps and with drawings on leather plaques stitched on to them.

Before I went to bed I walked over to the window to look at the lie of the land outside, a habit of mine in strange quarters. There was not a great deal to be seen, but the moonlight was strong enough to show me very clearly that the landscape was very different to that of my own homeland. Rather like another but enormous Bunda, the park lay spread out below, a dark splash over the rolling steppes, now shimmering softly in the light of the moon.

After looking out at this unfamiliar scene for a while I closed the window and turned back into the room. Undressing, I climbed into the bed which was covered by the Bunda. As I drew its soft fur gratefully up over my tired limbs and before my eyes closed in sleep I still had time to wonder what experiences might be awaiting me in this house: pleasant or disagreeable?

Then I fell asleep and everything that had already been in my life and everything for which I still so keenly longed faded together into unconsciousness.

The House in the Steppes

How long I slept I really do not know, but I do know that I slept neither soundly nor well. Perhaps over-tiredness was the cause. In any case, all night I wandered around on Vesuvius and I saw the Major, first dressed as a wanderer and sitting in Pompeii, and then in evening dress standing amidst the boulders on the mountain-side and looking for stones. Towards morning the whinnying of horses and the barking of dogs mingled with my dream. After that I slept quite soundly for a while and when I woke up it was broad daylight. From my bedroom I looked out into the main chamber where the weapons and the clothing were hanging. The rays of the early morning sun came through the windows, and outside the park was filled with the singing of birds. I got up and went to the windows. The heath was colourful again in the sunlight. I began to dress, but before I had quite finished there was a knock at the door. I opened it and my old friend came in.

For days I had been consumed with curiosity to know just what he would look like in these new surroundings, and now I saw that he looked very much as one would have expected of him, namely in complete harmony with them, so much so in fact that it was almost as though I had always known him just like this. On his upper lip there was the traditional long moustache, and his eyes were, if possible, brighter than ever. He was wearing the round, broad-brimmed hat and the long wide, white trousers of the countryside. It seemed so natural that he should be dressed like this that suddenly I could no longer remember what he looked like in evening dress. His Hungarian garb so took my fancy that my own well-worn German broadcloth that lay, still dusty from my journey, over a bench beneath the faded silk garments of some old Tartar seemed quite wretched by comparison. His jacket was shorter than we were accustomed to in Germany, but it certainly suited the whole style of his dress. He looked rather older, of course, and there were strands of white in his hair, and on his face were those fine, short lines that appear at last and indicate the passing of the years in men of culture. However, his general appearance was every bit as agreeable and engaging as before.

He welcomed me warmly, even affectionately, and after we had chatted for half an hour or so we were as intimate again as ever we had been. You might almost have thought, in fact, that we had not separated since our first meeting in Italy. Whilst completing my dressing I remarked that a trunk would arrive with the rest of my things, whereupon he proposed that until it did—or, indeed, throughout the whole period of my stay if I cared—I should wear Hungarian dress, and this I readily agreed to do. The necessary garments were soon brought and as I put them on he observed approvingly that he would see to it that I did not lack for variety whilst I was here. We then went down into the courtyard where his men, all with long moustaches and all similarly dressed, were waiting for us. As they led forward the horses for our morning ride they looked at us with such pleasure from under their bushy eyebrows, and there was such a general atmosphere of pleasant and cultivated well-being that my spirits rose at once and I was greatly heartened in these new and strange surroundings.

Accompanied by the great mastiff I had seen the previous evening we now made a tour of inspection of the Major's estate. As he showed me round it was soon clear that he took a keen and personal interest in everything that was going on, giving orders, commenting on this or that, and uttering words of praise where he felt they were due. We first rode through the park. It was a friendly, orderly wilderness with well-kept paths, and beyond it we rode out into fields that were a mass of tossing green. The only country in which I had ever seen such luxuriant green was England, but there the growth had seemed less strong and vigorous than it did here in these sun-drenched fields. We rode up a long incline to where the vineyards began. From this height I could see that the cultivated area spread far and wide over the landscape, the dark green relieved by many peach trees, whilst here and there, as at Maroshely, the white huts of labourers were picked out by the sun against the dark-green background of the vines. On the heath itself we saw his cattle grazing, a vast herd scattered around almost as far as eye could see. Then an hour's riding brought us to the stables and the sheepfolds. As we rode across the heath the Major pointed to a narrow, dark stretch of green cutting across the grey steppes to the west.

'They are the vineyards of Maroshely, where they lent you the horses yesterday,' he said.

We rode back a different way and on the other side of the estate he showed me the orchards, the gardens and the greenhouses. Before we came to them we rode through a rather barren and uninteresting stretch of land on which a great number of men were at work. In answer to my question he declared that they were beggars, tramps and vagabonds who had been persuaded to work for him in return for regular wages. They were engaged in draining marshland and in laying down a new road.

We returned to the house at midday and there we ate together with all the men and girls who were attached to the house. The meal was served under a large projecting roof forming a sort of veranda. Near by there was a large nut tree and one of the typical wells of the countryside. As we ate, a party of wandering gypsies grouped before the well played to us. I was not the only visitor. At our table was a youth who attracted my attention at once by his quite extraordinary beauty. He had brought letters to the house and after the meal he rode away again. I noticed that the Major treated him with great consideration and something very like affection.

The sun was very hot now and we spent the heat of the day in the cool rooms of the house. When evening came my host declared that the sunset on the heath was a sight worth seeing and he ordered the horses to be brought round for us. At the same time he advised me to wear a fur coat as a precaution against the fever of the plains, despite the fact that the still warm air seemed to make such a precaution unnecessary. We rode out to a suitable spot and there we waited for a while until the sun went down. The sunset was a wonderful spectacle indeed. The tremendous dome of the heavens covered the dark heath as though with a vast curtain of red and yellow flames and the glow was so great that everything on the ground seemed black and strange. A taller blade of grass would stand out against the light as though it were a beam and a passing animal was outlined against the fiery golden background like some dark mastodon, whilst modest juniper and blackthorn bushes looked like distant turrets and battlements. After a while the fresh, cold blue of the approaching night began to spread over the eastern horizon throwing dark shadows across the brilliance of the glowing sky.

In June, when the sun stands high in the heavens, the spectacle lasts for quite a while, and when we were already back at the house, and even after we had taken our evening meal and had chatted for some time, there was still a colourful glow in the west. In fact, when I stood at my window much later, just before retiring for the night—it was already past midnight—there was still a last vestige of yellow in the western sky although in the dark blue east the orange disc of the moon was already up.

As I stood there and looked out I decided that the next day, or the day after that, or whenever a convenient opportunity arose, I would ask the Major what it was exactly that he had referred to in his letter as having found here at last to keep him for ever in his own country.

He came to my room very early the next morning to ask me whether I would prefer to spend the day on my own or to share it with him. I could do whichever I pleased, today or on any other day of my stay. On any day that I wished to take part in the normal affairs of the household all I had to do was to rise at the sound of the house bell in the courtyard, which was rung every morning, and come down to the common table for breakfast. Should I, on the other hand, wish at any time to follow my own devices, then, if he were not there, his servants had been instructed to have horses ready for me, to provide me with anything I required, and to accompany me wherever I wished to go. However, should I ever have plans that would take me a long way from the house it would be as well if I would let him know beforehand so that he could advise me of any difficulties and perhaps warn me of any dangers that might be involved.

I was very grateful to him for his kindness and consideration and his readiness to assist me in everything, but I assured him that today, tomorrow and indefinitely I would prefer to spend my days with him. At the same time I should certainly let him know in good time of any change in my intentions.

When he had gone I got up, dressed and presented myself at the common table beneath the great roof for breakfast. The others had almost all finished their meal and were
already going off on the various tasks of the day, but the Major had waited for me and he sat there with me until I had
finished my breakfast. Saddled horses were then brought for
us and we set off. I did not ask where we were going or what
he intended to do; I just followed him wherever he rode.

It was no tour of inspection for my benefit this time as
it had been on the first day when he had showed me round
his estate and explained its running, and he declared that to-
day we would just attend to whatever matters that arose in
the ordinary course and he hoped that I would not be bored.
First we rode over to a wide expanse of meadowland where
haymaking was going on. The beautiful brown Hungarian
horses we were riding carried us spiritedly over the level
turf-like ground where the long grass had been cut. The Major dismounted to examine the quality of the hay in various
ricks and the man who held his horse in the meantime remarked that the hay was to be carried in that afternoon. Before we rode on the Major gave instructions that whilst the
grass was short a number of trenches should be dug here and
there, some to drain off surplus water, others to collect it.

Next we went to the greenhouses, which were not, as is
usually the case, near the house but in a very favourable
spot where a gentle slope offered protection in the mornings and at midday. Near the greenhouses was a small well-
kept stable where the Major and anyone who happened to be
with him could leave their horses if an extended stay in the
greenhouses was intended—sometimes, when visitors were
anxious to look over the houses thoroughly, the inspection
might take several hours. We left our horses in this stable
without having them unsaddled and went off to look at a
variety of plants which were being prepared for despatch
to fulfil orders. After that we entered a little office where
the administrative side of the business was attended to and
there the Major spent some time at a desk where various papers and correspondence were awaiting his attention. In the

meantime I looked around on my own with as much, or as little, understanding for what I saw as an inveterate traveller, who has seen many greenhouses in his time, manages, willy-nilly, to acquire. Later on, back at the house, I spent some time looking through that part of the Major's library which was devoted to horticultural matters and in consequence I was soon made to realize just how little I knew about the fundamentals of the science. The Major was certainly not exaggerating when he observed on another occasion:

'It is all quite fascinating, but if you want to do anything really worth while in such a complicated branch of horticulture, where one thing leads to another endlessly, you have to go into the matter very thoroughly indeed and constantly strive to outdo all your rivals at it.'

When the Major had finished his work in the office we continued our tour of inspection. We stopped to watch a number of women who were engaged in cleaning the leaves of camelia plants. In those days the camelia was quite a rare and therefore an expensive flower. The Major examined the plants that had already been wiped and made a comment or two. Then we walked along between many beds of fine white sand where seedlings were being grown, and from there on to ordinary beds where various kinds of plants and bushes were systematically cultivated. By this time we were on the far side of the gardens and there we found a lad waiting for us with the horses, which had been brought round from the stable to be ready for us. There was a large open space here where various soils were prepared and made up for particular uses. Donkeys were used to bring in earth in baskets from other localities, often from quite distant forests of fir trees, and this transport went on throughout the year except when the ground was frozen hard. Near by there was a row of great ovens for sterilizing the soil, and at a little distance there were great stacks of oak logs for use as fuel during the winter months.

Beyond the greenhouses, as I had already noticed, was the open heath and we now rode out into it. Our fine horses bore us along swiftly until soon the park was no more than a dark stretch on the horizon behind us and the great house a mere dot whilst all around the level plains rolled away and the scent of warm heather in the sun was in our nostrils. After a long gallop we fell in with the Major's herdsmen and came to a primitive hut of branches, hardly more than a recognizable spot that could be seen from afar and that served as a meeting-point. A fire of tough branches and the roots of juniper, blackthorn and other bushes was burning, or rather glowing, there and round it the herdsmen, who ate their meal early, at about eleven o'clock, were already engaged in preparing it. Sun-tanned men in short sleeves and the usual long, and in this case, rather dirty white trousers, crowded round the Major as we rode up. Their shaggy fur coats were scattered around on the ground. Others farther away had spotted the Major's arrival and now they came galloping up riding bare back on small, wiry ponies. They had neither saddles nor saddle cloths and their only bridle was often just a rope. They dismounted and, still holding their horses' heads, they joined the crowd around the Major, who had also dismounted and handed his horse to one of the men.

He asked questions and they answered him, but it was not only of their work that they talked and he seemed to know almost all of them by name. His manner towards them was very friendly, almost familiar, and their attitude to him was enthusiastic. As at home on our mountain pastures, the cattle here were kept out in the open throughout the summer months. They were long-horned beasts with white hides and they lived by cropping the grass and plants of the heath, which were, incidentally, of a pungency and flavour that our alpine herdsmen would hardly have credited. These herdsmen of the plains stayed out in the open with their cattle throughout the summer, and apart from the flimsy sort of construction I mentioned previously, and perhaps a mud hut or two, their only roof was the blue sky during the day and the bright stars of the pusta at night. Now they crowded round their master, the Lord of the Manor as he is called in these parts, and listened keenly to his instructions. When he remounted, one of the men, whose dark eyes sparkled under bushy eyebrows, held his horse's head whilst others, with long hair and thick drooping moustaches, bent down to hold his stirrup.

'Good-bye, men,' he called out cheerfully as we rode off. 'I shall be here again soon, and when our neighbours come over we'll spend an afternoon on the heath and eat with you.'

He had spoken in Hungarian of course and at my request he translated his words for me, adding:

'If you should ever feel inclined to come out here on your own to spend a day with the men and get to know their lives a bit better—take care of their dogs. They aren't usually as docile and friendly as they were today, and certainly not to strangers. In fact if you paid an unexpected visit it could go hard with you, so if you feel like riding out here at any time let me know beforehand so that I can go with you or arrange for one of the men to accompany you if I should be unable to.'

I had, in fact, taken particular note of the lean and shaggy dogs that had sat around us by the fire and behaved themselves so intelligently and so obediently. They seemed to know what was going on and to have their share in it. In all my travels I had never seen such impressive beasts.

We turned our horses' heads towards the house, for it was approaching midday and the time for the midday meal was drawing near. As we passed the place where the men were at work draining the marshland and laying out the new road the Major pointed to a field of wheat close by. The ears of grain seemed to be particularly full and heavy.

'Good fields like that have to produce the money to enable us to make improvements elsewhere,' he said. 'The hired men over there work on the marshland all the year through. They are paid daily and they prepare their food on the job in the open air. At nights they sleep in those wooden huts you can see over there. In winter when it begins to freeze we move them to the lower lying ground where nothing can be done in summer because of the stagnant water. They then cart stones and debris from the heath and the vineyards to make a firmer surface.'

I looked around and I could see the wooden huts to which he referred, and in various spots on the brow of the heath thin wisps of smoke were rising from where the day labourers were preparing their midday meal.

As we turned into the park the dogs ran up to welcome us, leaping up and dancing around our horses, and at that moment the bell in the courtyard began to ring to call us and the others to our midday meal. That afternoon was spent as usual in the house, though at five o'clock the Major set off along the avenue of poplars I had used to approach the house on the night of my arrival. I had no idea where he was going, or on what errand, and I spent the time he was away in looking through the books he was sending in to me in increasing numbers from his library. Although I had firmly determined to do so the evening before when I went to bed, I had found no opportunity of asking the Major what it was he had found here which had caused him to settle down so definitely, altogether abandoning his former mode of life.

The next day the Major had a good deal of writing to do and I spent the whole day with the horses in his stables and in getting to know his many servants.

The morning after that I went with him to the sheepfolds, which were situated a good two hours' ride away from the house, and there we spent the whole day. There were obviously a number of very capable men to look after this branch of his activities. They were devoted to their work and able to discuss it with him from all angles. It was here that I discovered that each of the various activities of his estate had its own separate accounting and that a surplus from one would be used to further the progress of the other. The sheep rearing, for example, was assisted in this way. A very careful accounting was kept and the Major's books would always provide an exact picture of the state of affairs prevailing in any branch of the estate's operations.

On another occasion we inspected the stud farm and then went out to the meadows where the horses of lesser value were looked after by his men in the same way as his cattle were looked after by his herdsmen.

In this way I gradually obtained a very good picture of all the activities on his estate, and the sum-total was not inconsiderable. I was astonished again and again at the great care and attention to details he showed in practical matters, for previously I had known him as interested only in literary and scientific affairs.

'As I see it,' he said to me on one occasion, 'we owe a duty to our land. Our country and our history are already old, but there is still a great deal left for us to do. The country is like a jewel—perhaps a more valuable jewel than you might think—but it still has to be given a proper setting. The whole world is striving to make the most of itself and we, too, have to play our part in the struggle. There are great latent capacities in our country but they must first be developed and brought out. I have no doubt that on your long way here you did not fail to observe those possibilities. These heaths make splendid agricultural land, and those hills with their bright stones that roll away to the blue mountains you can see in the north are full of hidden metals, whilst the soil itself offers rich nourishment to our vines. Two great streams flow through the land, but the sky above it is empty, so to speak, as though awaiting the fluttering of many triumphant flags. Different types of people inhabit the country and some of them are like children—they have first to be shown what to do before they will do it. Since I have lived amongst my people—over whom I have more rights than you might think—since I have worn their clothing, shared their customs and learned to know their ways, I have won their respect and affection, and in doing so I have found that good fortune I once searched for in vain in so many other lands.'

These few earnest words made it unnecessary for me to ask any direct questions concerning the wholly satisfying aim he had found in life and to which he had referred in his letters to me.

He had devoted himself in particular to improving the yield of the grain and he had experimented with various sorts. They now grew on all sides vigorously as a living tribute to the success of his activities. The cars were full and heavy and I was curious to know when the fields would be ripe for the reapers and the harvest brought in.

The single-minded devotion he showed to his lonely task often made me think of those sturdy early Romans, who also loved agricultural pursuits and who, in the early years of their history at least, were quite prepared to suffer the natural loneliness of the busy husbandman at work on his own lands.

How admirable and truly elemental is the destiny of the countryman! I thought. And how wonderful when he brings a ripe understanding to his tasks which can lift them from the rut and ennoble and refine them! In its simplicity and yet diversity and in its close contact with dispassionate nature it approaches the paradisal state.

Gradually I got to know the life on the Major's estate as though it had always been my own; I understood what was going on; I could watch the growth of the crops with an understanding eye and do my part to assist their progress. And soon the uneventful passage of the days in simple tasks so captured me that I felt happy and at peace with the world, forgetful of the towns I had left behind, as though I had turned my back on nothing of importance.

One day we were again on the heath amongst the horses and their guardians, and as it happened the latter were joined by the herdsmen who tended the cattle so that an unusually large number of the Major's men were gathered around us. As we drove home—this time we were not on horseback but in a broad-based carriage whose wheels rolled safely over the heath as it was drawn along by a pair of fine horses in full harness—the Major referred to his men.

'I could lead those men into battle if I cared to place myself at their head,' he declared. 'They are absolutely devoted to me, and so are all the servants and labourers around the house. They would let themselves be cut into pieces rather than have anything happen to me. And if I add those who are subject to me by feudal right and are equally devoted to me—as they have shown on many occasions—I could muster quite a large army of men who love me. And remember:

I did not come to them until my hair was going grey, and after long years of forgetfulness. What must it be like to lead hundreds of thousands of such men and guide their steps towards a noble aim ? Once they trust a leader they are generally like children and they will follow loyally wherever they are led—to good or evil.'

After a while he spoke again:

'At one time I imagined that I would be an artist or a scholar, but then I realized that such men must have a deep and earnest message for humanity, a message to arouse enthusiasm, to make men greater and nobler. The scholar at least must discover and reveal things that will further the material well-being of humanity and improve the means to attain it. But in the one case and the other the man himself must first possess a big and simple heart. As I was convinced that I possessed no such thing, I let my opportunities pass by—and now it is too late.'

As he spoke these words it seemed to me as though a shadow passed over his face, and at that moment it was as though he looked out into the world with that same ecstatic reverie I had known in him in former years when, sitting idly on the Epomeo, we had talked together of the innumerable wishes and dreams of youth whilst all around us the heavens were almost solemnly blue and the sea glittered in the sun below us. And suddenly I wondered whether the happiness he had thought to find here was altogether so complete after all.

This was the only occasion throughout our whole acquaintanceship that he had made any reference to his past life.

Before that he had never given even the slightest indication. For my part I had never asked any questions, nor did I do so now. A man who has travelled widely learns to treat others with consideration and never to refer to the intimate personal affairs of a man's life, for they are never revealed except voluntarily.

I had already been with the Major for quite a time now, and very gladly too, for I had come to take a great interest in the management of his estate and I had often taken an active hand in the work connected with it. Whilst not so engaged I had devoted myself to keeping a diary of my travels and my experiences. As a result of my stay at Unwar there was now one thing of which I felt fairly confident: as simple and active as the life was that the Major led here, there was some faintly disturbing element present which had not yet been altogether resolved, and at the same time a certain sadness which, in such a man, expressed itself in serene and earnest resignation.

In all other matters that arose during our life together at Unwar he was frank and open with me and there was no question of reserve or dissimulation. I often visited him in his study, where we would spend the heat of the day or the cool of the evening by candlelight before retiring for the night, chatting about a great variety of matters. On his desk there was a small portrait of a young woman in the early twenties. To me the most interesting feature of this portrait was that although the artist had no doubt done his best to gloss over the fact, it was not the portrait of a beautiful young woman but rather that of a plain one. But there was vitality in the face and strength of character, too. The dark complexion and the shape of the forehead were unusual and the eyes were proud and untamed. It was certainly the portrait of a determined woman.

It was not difficult to imagine that this young woman must have played some role in his former life, and the sight of that portrait made me wonder—as I had wondered during our stay in Italy together—why such a man had never married. But on principle I had not asked him then and for the same reason I made no comment now. The fact that the picture was there openly on his writing desk meant nothing, for none of his people ever came into the room. If any of his men had anything to say to him and he was in his study they had to wait in an ante-room where their entrance rang a little bell which announced their presence. He also never received visitors in his study in the ordinary way and it was therefore an indication of some intimacy that I was allowed to enter the room. In fact it was perhaps this signal mark of his confidence and trust in me that saved me from pondering and speculating.

Harvesting had now begun and I shall never forget the cheerful, happy days that accompanied it. Now and again the Major had to visit places in the neighbourhood and he always invited me to accompany him. There are few countries in Europe where the distances between the inhabited centres are so great, but we would cover them in a comparatively short time either on horseback or driving fast over the heath in a light carriage. For one such journey the Major dressed himself in the close-fitting national costume of Hungary and at his side he wore a sabre. The handsome garb suited him very well. It was to a meeting of the local administrative body that we went and there he delivered a speech in Hungarian. It was always my endeavour in whatever land I came to learn as much of the language as I could and as quickly as possible. I had therefore picked up quite a little Hungarian from the Major's men and from everyone else with whom I came into contact, with the result that I was able to understand quite a lot of what he said. The reception accorded to his words varied from warm approval and admiration to no less warm disapproval. On the way back he translated the whole speech into German for me. That evening he once again wore evening dress and he was as I had known him in Italy. Most of the others present had put off their Hungarian costumes and were also in ordinary European evening dress. I accompanied him on other journeys and I learned that there were four estates in the neighbourhood, of which the Major's was one. A few years back the owners of these estates had agreed that they would work together to raise agricultural standards and improve the quality of the local crops. This they proposed to do by setting a practical example on their own estates and encouraging others to follow it, which they would most likely do when they observed that it led to prosperity and a better life for all. This association of estates had developed its own rules and from time to time its members came together to discuss whatever matters happened to arise. As yet only these four large estates were actually members of the association, but a number of smaller landowners had already begun to follow the example of their bigger neighbours without formally joining the association. Those landowners and farmers of the neighbourhood who were not members of the association were at liberty to attend its meetings, listen to the proceedings and ask for advice and information, the only condition being that they should give notice in good time of their intention to be present, and, as I saw when I went to such a meeting, very many of them took advantage of this privilege. This particular meeting took place on another estate about four hours' ride from Unwar. It belonged to a local worthy named Gömör, who was a member of the association. The only members present at this meeting were the Major and this Gömör, but it was well attended by an audience of interested parties who had come to listen to the proceedings.

I had already got to know this Gömör quite well and I had visited his estate on two previous occasions. On the second I had even stayed there for a few days.

When the harvesting was almost over and there was less to attend to, the Major broached a new project.

'We shall be having more time to ourselves now,' he said, 'and next week we will ride over to my neighbour Brigitta Maroshely's estate on a visit. When you meet her I think you will agree with me that she is the most wonderful woman in the world.'

Two days after this earnest remark he made me acquainted with Brigitta Maroshely's son, who happened to have come over to Unwar for some reason. It was the handsome youngster who had eaten at our table on the first day after my arrival and whom I had noticed in particular at the time because of his exceptional good looks. This time he remained at Unwar throughout the day and went with us on our visits to various parts of the estate. He was, as I had already noted, still very young indeed, little more than a boy and hardly even a stripling as yet. I took to him at once. His eye was dark and amiable and when he sat on horseback there was something at the same time so vigorous and yet so modest about his demeanour that my heart went out to him. I had once had a very good friend, whose fate had been to go to an early grave, and Gustave—for such was the name of Brigitta Maroshely's son—reminded me of him very strongly.

Since the Major had praised Brigitta Maroshely so highly, and now that I had made the acquaintance of her son, I was very anxious to meet the mother in person.

Whilst I was the guest of Gömör I had learnt something of the Major's past. Gömör, like so many of the people I met here, was of a frank and open disposition, and he spoke to me freely and without prompting of what he knew. The Major, it appeared, was not of a local family at all. His parents had been very rich and from his youth he had travelled around constantly. No one really knew where his travels had taken him or in whose service he had attained the rank of Major. In his youth he had never been to Unwar at all, having first come there only a few years previously. However, once there, he had settled down and joined the association of those landowners who styled themselves the friends of agriculture. At that time the association had consisted of two members only: he, Gömör, and Brigitta Maroshely. In fact, in those days it had not really been an association at all, and the rules and the holding of formal meetings was to come only later. It had all started because two good neighbours, he, Gömör, and Brigitta Maroshely, had talked the matter over and decided to work together to improve their property in this rather barren part of the country. Incidentally, the initiative in the matter had come from Brigitta Maroshely.

Although a very agreeable and intelligent woman, he went on, she was not beautiful, and her husband, a frivolous scamp to whom she had been married when she was very young, had soon left her and never returned. After this desertion she had come to Maroshely, which was the name of the estate, with her son, who had then been only a very small child. She had taken over the management of the estate as efficiently as any man and soon introduced new methods and improvements. In fact, she had begun to dress like a man and she rode astride like a man. She worked hard herself from morning to night and she kept a firm rein on her servants and her labourers. She had shown what persistent hard work can do and she had achieved wonders on what had been little more than a stony waste. He, Gömör, had got to know her well and he had followed her example and introduced her methods on his own estate, and up to the present he had seen no cause to regret it.

When the Major had first come to settle in Unwar he had never ridden over to Maroshely to visit his neighbour, but when he had already been at Unwar for a number of years Brigitta Maroshely had fallen seriously ill. She had been at death's door and then the Major had ridden over to Maroshely and attended to her until she was well again. From that time on he had visited her frequently. Her recovery under his care had been so remarkable that at the time there had been a good deal of talk of animal magnetism, at which the Major was said to be an adept. However, no one had known anything for certain about his methods. In any case, an unusually close and intimate friendship had developed between the two. Brigitta Maroshely was certainly worthy of the profoundest feelings of friendship, but whether of the passionate attachment the Major had conceived for the already ageing and far from beautiful woman was another matter. But passion was undoubtedly the right word to describe the Major's feelings for her and everyone who knew them both could plainly see it. The Major would undoubtedly marry Brigitta if he could, and he was obviously deeply grieved at not being able to do so. Nothing was known about the husband's whereabouts or his fate and there was therefore no possibility of a divorce, nor could his death be assumed. It said a good deal for Brigitta Maroshely's qualities that she, whose husband had once so irresponsibly left her, should now be sought after by such a serious wooer.

Such was the story Gömör told me about the affairs of Brigitta Maroshely and the Major, and it made me more than ever anxious to meet her. Whilst out visiting I saw her son again on one or two occasions, and then the day came which had been fixed for our ride over to Maroshely to visit his mother.

The night before as I lay in bed and the chirping of myriads of crickets filled my drowsy ear before I fell asleep my thoughts dwelt on her and all I had heard. And when I fell asleep she appeared in my dreams. I stood once again on the heath before the strange rider who had lent me the horse and the escort to take me to Unwar and her beautiful eyes held me so in thrall that I was rooted to the spot and aware that I was condemned to spend the rest of my days there on the heath, unable to stir. But then my dream ceased and I fell into an untroubled sleep to wake up feeling fresh and vigorous the next morning. After breakfast our horses were brought round and in my heart I was delighted to know that at last I was to see face to face the woman who had so occupied my thoughts, even to appearing in my dreams in the night.

A Past in the Steppes

Before I describe how we came to Maroshely, how I made the acquaintance of Brigitta and how I came to be so often on her estate after that, I must first tell something at least of her earlier life, for without that it would be impossible to understand what follows. How I obtained such a detailed knowledge of the circumstances which are about to be described will result naturally from my relationship to the Major and to Brigitta Maroshely and develop as my story goes along. It is not necessary that I should reveal beforehand what I myself did not learn prematurely but from the unfolding of the events themselves.

The human race possesses an extraordinary and wonderful quality which we know as beauty. We are all attracted by a felicity in appearance though we are not always able to say just in what the attraction consists. Beauty is everywhere around us. It lies in the eye of the beholder. Yet sometimes it is not present in features which seem formed according to all the canons that normally produce it. Sometimes beauty goes unperceived because it blossoms in the desert, or because the seeing eye has not yet lighted upon it. And often it is praised and near idolized where in reality it is lacking. But where a heart beats high in ecstasy and passion, and where two hearts beat as one, it is ever present, or the heart would fail and the love of twin souls perish.

It is a strange flower and often it blooms in unlikely places, but, whatever the soil, once it burgeons it can hardly be destroyed. Remove it from one spot and it will blossom again in another, and often in the least considered place. It is proper to mankind alone and it magnifies the man who kneels before it, pouring into his trembling and ecstatic heart all the things that make the life of man worth while. To have it not, or know it not, is a tragedy, and he in whom no other eye can perceive it is an object of pity. Even the heart of a mother can turn away from a child in whom she cannot—or can no longer—divine even the faintest shimmer of its glory.

And so it was with the child Brigitta. When she was born her mother had no feelings for her child. To her it was not the helpless, appealing little creature that calls out all the love and tenderness in a normal mother's heart. And later when the child lay amidst the snow-white linen in its beautiful gilded cot its face was clouded over because of this deprivation and it was as though a wicked fairy had breathed over it. Almost unwittingly the mother would turn her glance away to where her two other little children played together on the deep, rich carpet. They were the vessels of beauty to her.

When strangers came they neither praised nor criticized the new-born child but turned their attention to its sisters. And so the child grew up. The father often went through the room indifferently on his affairs, and when the mother sometimes embraced and fondled the other children in despairing ardour she did not observe the dark eyes of Brigitta as they stared at her unwinkingly as though the small child already understood and resented the slight it put upon her. When the child cried her wants were attended to; when she remained quiet she was left alone. The others had their own affairs that interested them and the child lay there, staring at the gilt decorations on her cot or at the intricate patterns on the wallpaper.

When her limbs grew stronger and her cot was no longer the one place in which she stayed, she would sit in a corner and play with her bricks and utter strange sounds she had heard from no one. As her games became more complicated her rebellious eyes would often bear that look that boys have when they intend some forbidden thing. If her sisters ever tried to join in her games she would reject them roughly, even striking them. And when, in a belated surge of love and pity, her mother would take her into her arms and weep over her the child would go stiff and cry and struggle to escape from the clinging arms around her. Because of this rejection and frustration the mother now grew more loving, but also more embittered. She did not realize that when the first small soft roots had sought the warm soil of mother love and found themselves rebuffed they had turned in on themselves and found an obstinate hold in the stoniness of a lonely heart.

And now the stony waste spread still farther.

As the children grew up and the period of fine clothes began, those for Brigitta were always thought to be good enough for her. But the clothes of her sisters were altered and adjusted again and again before they were finally considered perfect. Great care was taken to teach the other children how to behave and they were praised when their conduct was pleasing. Brigitta was not even blamed, although she often creased her clothes and made them dirty.

When the time came for learning lessons and the mornings were devoted to them, Brigitta would sit there staring at book or map with the only beautiful feature she possessed: her dark, glowing eyes. And if the teacher suddenly asked her a question she would start, as though out of a reverie, and not know what to answer. During the long evenings, and at other times when the family was in the drawing-room and she was not missed, she would lie at full length on the floor, sprawling on books or pictures, or on torn cards her sisters no longer wanted. And all the while a fantastic but crippled world festered in her heart. The library door was never locked and, although no one suspected it, she had read half her father's books, though most of them she could not as yet understand. Now and again pieces of paper were found lying around with strange and wild drawings on them, and these she must have made.

As the young girls began to become young ladies Brigitta was like some strange plant in a conventional bed. Her sisters were now soft-fleshed beautiful creatures, made to grace a drawing-room, but Brigitta was strong and slim. Her strength was almost that of a youth, and if her sisters teased her, or wanted to embrace her affectionately, she would put them away firmly with her strong slim arms. Manual labour attracted her and often she would work until beads of sweat stood out on her forehead. She took no music lessons as her sisters did, but she rode a horse with spirit and as well as any youth. Often she would lie in the grass, wearing her best clothes, talking to herself and declaiming to the silent bushes.

It was about this time that her father began to make her reproaches for her wayward and obstinate behaviour. Even when she did talk she would sometimes fall silent suddenly and her mood would become sullen and resentful. It was no use her mother's making encouraging signs to her or expressing helplessness and bitter despair by wringing her hands; her daughter still remained silent. On one occasion her angry father so far forgot himself as to chastise her, the grown girl, because she refused to go into the drawing-room when her presence was desired there. She just looked at him with hot, dry eyes, and still refused to go. Whatever he did would have made no difference; she would have remained unmoved.

If there had been just one person around her with an understanding eye for her hidden self, just one who could see the beauty that was there, just one person for whom she could have felt something beyond contempt and resentment... But there was no one. The others could not help her and there was nothing she could do for them.

The family lived in town and had always done, and there they led a life of brilliance and fashion. As the daughters grew up and became young women of marriageable age, reports of their beauty spread and soon many people were coming to the house on their account, and the social gatherings and entertainments became even more numerous and more brilliant than before. The heart of more than one young man beat higher and longed for possession of one of the treasures the house contained. But the girls were unmoved; as yet they were too young to understand such things. However, they gave themselves up gladly to the pleasure such parties brought with them, and the ordering of a new gown and all the preliminaries of a party would occupy their rapt attention for days in advance. Not so Brigitta. In any case, as the youngest she was never consulted, as though she "were still too young to know and understand anything about such matters. Sometimes she was present on such social occasions and then she would always wear a full-skirted black silk dress she had made herself, but usually she avoided company and remained in her own room, and no one knew how she occupied her time there. A number of years passed in this way and then one day a certain young man who had already caused quite a fluttering in various circles appeared in the town. His name was Stephen Murai and he had been brought up on his father's country estate. When his formal education was completed he was sent out on the Grand Tour in preparation for taking his place in the select society of his own country. It was on his return that he came to the capital, where Brigitta and her family lived. Before long he became the main subject of conversation in society. Some praised his intelligence and others praised his good manners, his charm and his modesty. And many people declared that they had never seen anyone quite so handsome as this young newcomer. But, of course, there were those who preferred malice and slander, and they said that there was something wild and arrogant about him. You could see quite plainly, they said, that he had been brought up in the country. He was also proud, they said, and, if it came to the point, probably deceitful. But one way or the other, more than one young woman who had not yet had the opportunity was very anxious to make his acquaintance when she heard of his reputation.

Brigitta's father knew this young man's family quite well, and as a young man, when he too had travelled a good deal, he had often stayed on their estate, though later, when he settled down in town for good, he had rather lost touch with them. He knew that at that time this family had been wealthy and now he made discreet inquiries about their present state, finding, to his satisfaction, that they were now wealthier than ever, for the simple life they led on their country estates had caused their fortunes to increase still further. Should this young man prove personally acceptable, therefore, he would obviously make a very suitable candidate for the hand of one of the girls. It was quite obvious, of course, that in view of the young man's expectations other mothers and fathers would be moved by similar ideas and so Brigitta's father lost no time but promptly invited the young man to visit the house.

This Stephen Murai did on a number of occasions, but at first Brigitta did not meet him because for some time she had practically given up her in any case rare appearances in the drawing-room. However, at about this time she accepted an invitation to a social gathering at the house of an uncle. This was unusual, but as a younger girl she had sometimes stayed with this uncle and found his company agreeable. She was therefore present that evening and she sat there in her usual black silk dress watching what was going on around her. She was also wearing a headdress she had made for herself. It was not the fashion to wear such a headdress and her sisters found it unbecoming, even ugly, but, in fact, it suited her dark complexion very well.

Many guests were present and when she casually looked towards a little group not far away from where she was sitting she noticed that a young man with dark, romantic eyes was looking at her. Modestly she looked away at once, but a little later she observed that the young man was again looking at her. It was Stephen Murai.

About a week later her father gave a ball and Stephen Murai was invited. He arrived when most of the other guests were already present and the dancing had already begun. The gentlemen were just taking their partners for the second dance and looking around he saw Brigitta. He went up to her immediately and asked her respectfully for the honour of the dance, but she refused, saying that she had never learned to dance. He then bowed silently and went away. Brigitta sat down on a couch behind a table and watched the glittering scene around her. Murai chatted happily with various people and danced with some of the young ladies. That evening he seemed more than usually agreeable and courteous to everyone. At last the ball came to an end and the guests departed.

Brigitta went up to her room—it had cost her a great deal of pleading and persistence to persuade her parents to let her have a room to herself in which she could be alone as she desired. As she undressed now—she could not bear to have a maid around her—she looked into the mirror and studied her dark-complexioned face in its frame of jet black curls. When she went to bed—it was not a soft couch, but firm, as she liked it—she drew up the white linen sheets and lay down with her slim arms behind her head and stared with sleepless eyes at the ceiling.

Other parties followed, and now Brigitta was always there and so was Stephen Murai. He continued to pay attention to her, greeting her respectfully, and when she rose to go he would always be at hand to help her with her shawl or give her her fan. Once she had left the room it was not long before the wheels of Stephen Murai's carriage sounded in the courtyard below as he was driven home.

This went on for some time until one evening she was again at a party given by her uncle. It was a warm evening and it was hot in the ballroom so Brigitta went out on to the balcony through the open French windows. Hearing a step behind her she turned and found that Stephen Murai had followed her. Standing there on the balcony away from the lights they talked of unimportant matters, but there was an unusual timidity in his voice. He referred to the night then and said that it was unjust to speak harshly of the darkness. On the contrary, it was a kind and lovely thing and it soothed and comforted the anxious heart. Then he fell silent and she fell silent with him. After a while they went back into the ballroom and he stood for a long time by himself at a window.

When Brigitta went home that night she undressed in her room, slowly discarding one piece of finery after the other, and putting on her nightdress. Then once again she looked at herself in the mirror, for a long time. Tears welled to her eyes and soon she was weeping uncontrollably. They were the first tears she had ever wept in her life and now they ran down her cheeks freely as though she were making up for all the bitter but unshed tears of her life. She had sunk to the floor and she sat there crouched down with her feet under her and cried her heart out as though relief would come when she could cry no more. It was a place where she often sat crouched in reverie and by chance there was a picture on the floor there, a child's picture and it showed one brother sacrificing himself for the other. Impulsively, and hardly knowing why, she picked it up and pressed it to her lips until it was creased from her kisses and wet from her tears.

At last she ceased to weep, but although the candles had burnt low she still crouched there on the floor before her mirror like a heart-broken child that has cried itself out and feels relief. Her hands lay crossed and motionless in her lap and the ribbons and pleats of her nightdress were damp from her tears and hung disconsolately over her ripening bosom. There she remained sunk in reverie, but after a long while she sighed deeply once or twice as though drawing new breath into her body. Then she passed her hand over her eyes, rose and went to bed. Lying there by the faint glow of a night light she had placed behind a small screen after having put out the candles she murmured to herself incredulously:

'It can't be true. It can't be true.'

And then she fell asleep.

When she met Stephen Murai again after that nothing seemed to have changed outwardly between them, but he sought her company more than ever and there was now something shy and almost hesitant in his manner. He said very little to her and she gave him no encouragement, not even the slightest.

There were many opportunities for him to speak to her alone, but he let them all pass unutilized until one day another arose and then he summoned up courage and spoke. He said that he felt that she was not very amiably disposed towards him, and if that were really so all he asked was that she should allow herself to get to know him better then he might not prove entirely unworthy of her attention. Perhaps, after all, he had qualities, or could develop them, which would win her respect... her respect at least, if not something he would desire a thousand times more earnestly.

'No, Stephen,' she answered. 'It is not that I am not well disposed towards you. Oh, no! Far from it. But there is one thing I must beg of you. Do not seek my hand. Do not, I beg of you, for if you do you will most surely have cause to regret it.'

'But why, Brigitta? Why do you say that?' the young man asked in amazement.

It was a moment or two before she replied and then she spoke slowly:

'Because no love but the very deepest would be at all acceptable to me. You see, I know that I am not beautiful, and just because of that I would demand a love greater than that you could feel for the most beautiful girl in the world. How deep such a love would have to be I cannot tell, but I feel that it would have no limit and no end. And now you know how impossible it is that you should pay court to me. You are the only one who has ever taken it for granted that I even had a heart at all, and because of that I would never deceive you.'

Perhaps she would have said more, but at that moment others approached and he saw that her lips were trembling as though in pain.

It is clear that far from discouraging Stephen Murai such words were calculated to increase his ardour. He began to worship her almost as though she were an angel of light and always he ignored the greater beauties so willingly around him, looking instead beyond them in the hope of meeting her eyes. And so it went on until in her breast the dark irresistible power began to stir and cause her arid heart to blossom and tremble. It was soon impossible for either of them to conceal such feelings altogether. Those around them began incredulously to suspect the unbelievable and when at last they were convinced their astonishment knew no bounds.

For his part Stephen Murai took no pains to conceal his feelings for Brigitta. On the contrary, he seemed anxious that all the world should know. One day as they stood alone in a room from which they could hear in the distance the sound of the music the company had come together to enjoy, he took her hand and drew her to him wordlessly. She made no attempt to resist the gentle pressure and their faces came closer and closer together until she felt his lips on hers and softly answered his kiss.

It was the first time in her life that she had ever kissed a living soul, not even her mother or her sisters. And many years later Murai declared that never in his life either before or since had he experienced such pure and deep emotion as he did the first time those lonely, untouched lips met his.

With this first kiss the barrier that had been between the two was gone. There was no further hindrance to their union. Within a few days the two were openly affianced and Brigitta was the intended bride of the man who had been so widely and so earnestly sought after. Both families readily gave their approval to the match and a serener relationship developed between the two young people. A warm and heartening glow gradually arose in the lonely heart of the neglected girl, and then steadily developed into something rich and gay.

The instinct that had drawn Stephen Murai to her had not deceived him. Her character was stronger and purer than that of most women, and because her heart had never been burdened by premature thoughts and imaginings of love, real love, now that it had come, could flourish in it all the more strongly. The intimate association that now developed between the two was more than usually delightful to him. Because she had always been alone she had built up a world of her own into which no one else had entered, but now he was privileged to do so and it was something new and strange and sweet that had previously belonged to her alone. Her personality began to flower richly before his eyes and he gratefully recognized the warmth and profundity of her love, which rose like a stream of pure gold as though between banks that had long been deserted. The hearts of others were divided amongst a great many things and a great many people, but hers had remained whole, and as he had been the only one to recognize its very presence so now he was the only one to possess it.

Time passed on light and delicate wings and he lived in joy and elation throughout the days of their betrothal. At last came their wedding day and at the church portals after the solemn ceremony Stephen Murai took his silent bride into his arms and lifted her into the carriage that was to take them to their new home.

The two young people had decided to live in town, and thanks to his father's generosity Stephen Murai had been able to take a fine house and furnish it magnificently. His father had long been a widower living alone on his country estate and never coming to the capital; but for his son's wedding he made the journey. Brigitta's father and mother were there too, together with her sisters, her favourite uncle and a number of other close relations. Both Murai's father and Brigitta's had desired that the marriage should be solemnized in great state and so it had been and afterwards there was a splendid reception for all the wedding guests.

When the last guests had departed, Stephen Murai led his bride through the brilliantly lit reception rooms to their own private apartments and there he sat alone with the girl who until then had had only one room that she could really call her own and who was now his wife.

'How beautiful everything was, Brigitta! And how wonderfully everything has come to pass! I knew the first moment I saw you. Something told me at once that you were a woman to whom I could not remain indifferent. But I did not realize at once that I must either love you or hate you for ever. How happy I am that it is love and not hate!'

Brigitta made no reply, but she held his hand in hers and her fine dark eyes looked serenely around her.

After a while Murai called the servants and ordered them to clear away all signs of the wedding reception, to extinguish the unnecessary lights and to turn the festive house into the living place they were now to occupy together. When this was done the servants were sent to their quarters and the first night descended on the new home and on the new family of two who had shared it for but a few hours.

From then on Stephen Murai and his bride lived almost wholly in their own home, visiting the houses of others only rarely. When they had first made each other's acquaintance they had always been in the company of others, and even during their engagement they had been together only in public. Now they retired gladly into the privacy of their own home and neither felt that anything outside themselves or outside their walls was necessary to their happiness.

Although the house had been well furnished and lavishly equipped, there was still a great deal to be done to make it exactly as they wanted it, an addition here, an improvement there, a re-arrangement elsewhere. They thought over what was still to be done, consulted each other on all points and discussed what was still to be obtained, until in this way their surroundings were gradually ordered to their liking and their guests were received in an atmosphere of domestic comfort and simplicity which was at the same time refined and beautiful.

Within a year of their marriage Brigitta bore her husband a son, and this new marvel kept them more than ever in their own home. Brigitta was taken up with the care for her child, and Murai now had his affairs to attend to, for his father had handed over part of the estate and this Murai now administered from the town.

When the boy was old enough not to need quite the same constant attention, and when Murai had put his own affairs so far into order that they no longer needed his every spare moment, he began to take his wife out again; into society, to public places, to the theatre and so on. On such occasions Brigitta noticed that he treated her if possible with even greater consideration and more marked affection than he did at home and her heart moved to him in gratitude for his understanding.

In the following spring he took her and the boy away into the country and when they returned in the autumn he proposed that they should now live in the country rather than the town, making their home on one of his estates. After all, he declared, it was much more beautiful in the country than in the town and life was, on the whole, more agreeable there. Brigitta agreed and so they went into the country to live.

Once they were there Murai settled down to the life of a country gentleman on his estate, in which he now took a deep interest, developing it and introducing many changes for the better. His chief recreation was shooting and he often went out alone with his gun, sometimes on foot and sometimes on horseback. It was thus that fate led him to make the acquaintance of another woman, a being totally different to anything he had known before. It was on one such shooting expedition that he first saw her.

His horse was picking its way carefully down a wooded slope when suddenly he turned his head involuntarily and his eyes met those of a beautiful woman who was regarding him through the foliage of the surrounding bushes. They were like the eyes of some shy and untamed gazelle, and before he could take a second and closer look they were gone. The woman was also on horseback and in a moment she had turned her horse and galloped away across the heath.

Her name was Gabrielle, he discovered, and she was the only daughter of an old Count who had his estate in the neighbourhood. She had, like him, been brought up in the country and she was a wild creature, for her father had allowed her to do as she pleased, believing that in this way she would best develop her natural qualities and not grow up to be an animated doll like the women of the town, for whom the Count had nothing but contempt. Gabrielle's beauty was renowned throughout the neighbourhood, but no word of it had as yet come to Murai's ears, for he had never lived on this estate before and quite recently he had been travelling to his other estates.

A few days later the two met again, at the very same spot. After that they met often and became acquainted. They asked no questions of each other and they were not curious to know who they were or where they came from. They just accepted each other, and the girl, unsophisticated and ingenuous, laughed, joked and teased Murai, urging him on to ride wild and daring races with her and galloping along madly at his side, an untamed and heavenly enigma. He fell in gaily with her high spirits and usually let her win. One day when they were racing wildly over the heath and she was too exhausted and out of breath to speak she could bring him to a halt only by grasping repeatedly at his bridle. He reined in his horse and dismounted. As he lifted her out of the saddle she leaned against him and whispered softly that she was defeated. Her stirrup leather needed adjustment and as he put it right she stood against a tree, breathless, but glowing with life and vitality. When he straightened himself he seized her impulsively and pressed her to him fiercely. Then, without waiting to see whether she was pleased or angry, he leapt into the saddle and galloped off.

It was sheer high spirits and the impulse of a moment that had made him act so, but as he held her there was an indescribable ecstasy in his heart, and as he rode back his mind was filled with thoughts of her soft cheeks, her sweet breath and her sparkling eyes.

After that they no longer sought each other's company, and when by chance they met again in the house of a neighbour they both flushed a deep red. Murai then went away to visit one of his other estates a long way off, and there he stayed for some time in a fever of reorganization and rearrangement.

Brigitta was aware of what had happened and her heart went numb. A bitter feeling of shame arose in her bosom and when she went about the house on her affairs it was as though a dark shadow were moving through the rooms. But at last she ruthlessly crushed the gnawing pain in her heart and made her decision.

When Murai returned from the storm of activity on his distant estate she went to him in his room and gently proposed that they should part. It took him by surprise and shocked him deeply, but he argued with her, pleaded with her, begged her to change her mind. In vain. All she would say was: 'I warned you that you would have cause to regret it if you married me. I warned you that you would regret it.'

At last he sprang to his feet, seized her hands and declared with deep emotion: 'Woman, I hate you more than words can say. I hate you.'

She made no reply to his impassioned outburst but just looked at him with dry, reddened eyes.

He packed his trunk and sent it on ahead and three days afterwards, towards evening, he left the house in his travelling clothes. When he had gone she threw herself to the floor and lay there as she had once lain in the grass declaiming to the silent bushes the feelings that filled her heart. But now they were feelings of pain and humiliation and the scalding tears ran from her eyes unchecked. They were the last tears she shed for the man she loved so much and after that her eyes were dry.

In the meantime he galloped wildly over the heath, and a hundred times he was sorely tempted to draw the saddle pistol from its holster and blow his fevered brains out. On his way, and whilst it was still daylight, he had passed Gabrielle standing on the balcony of her father's house and looking out. He did not even raise his eyes but rode on past her without a sign of recognition.

Six months later he sent back formal agreement to the divorce and his consent to his wife's retaining the boy. Perhaps he felt that the child would be better taken care of in her hands, or perhaps his old love for her made him unwilling to deprive her of the last dear thing she possessed. After all, for him the whole world now lay open again. At the same time he made generous provision for both her and the boy, sending her all the necessary documents containing the arrangements. This was the first sign she had received from him since his departure, and it was the last. Nor did she see him again. She learned later from his lawyer that the funds he needed for himself had been transferred to a banking house at Amsterdam. More she never learned.

Not long after this parting Brigitta's father, mother and two sisters all died within a very short space of time. And a little while after that Murai's father, who was already an old man, died too. Brigitta was now completely alone in the world with her child.

Far away from the capital she owned an estate in a barren part of the country where she was unknown. The house and the estate were known as Maroshely and it was the place from which her own family took its name. She decided to go there where she could live unknown to the rest of the world and this she did, resuming her maiden name.

As a child when they had given her, perhaps out of pity, a beautiful doll, she had played with it happily for a while, but then discarded it in favour of things that were dearer to her, simple things, strangely shaped sticks and stones. Now she took with her to Maroshely the greatest treasure she possessed, her son, abandoning all else. And there she watched over him, caring for him devotedly, with eyes only for him and his needs. But as he grew older and his own world extended so did hers. She began to pay more attention to the running of her estate and to the development of the barren heathlands around her. She put on man's clothing, rode astride as she had done in her youth, and began to appear more freely amongst her people.

As soon as the boy could ride a horse he went everywhere with her, and the vigorous, creative, longing soul of

the mother now gradually flowered in the son. Her interests and her activities grew wider and a paradise of creative
activity surrounded her and rewarded her efforts. The bare
hills around grew green with the vines and gushing streams
watered the plains until what had been a stony waste became a rich and heroic poem of human effort. And like all
real poetry it brought its own blessings.

Others followed her shining example and an association
of like-minded landowners grew up to carry her efforts still
further. Even those who lived farther away were now moved
to enthusiasm and emulation and on the blind and barren
heathlands there were increasing signs of vigorous human
activity as though a friendly eye were opening in the wasteland.

Brigitta had lived and worked at Maroshely for fifteen
years when my friend the Major came to his neglected estate at Unwar and elected to settle down for the rest of his
life there where he had never lived before, and where, he assured me, he learned application and persistence from this
strange woman to whom he was soon deeply attracted by
the belated affection I have previously recorded.

A Present in the Steppes

The Major and I rode over to Maroshely. Brigitta was really the woman I had seen on horseback on the day of my arrival. Her friendly smile showed that she recalled our short
acquaintance and I blushed, remembering my unfortunate
attempt to give her money. There were no other guests present and the Major introduced me as an old acquaintance of
his travels in whose company he had spent a good deal of
time—an acquaintance, he added, who was about, he flattered himself to think, to develop into a friend. I was very
gratified—and it was really no small thing for me—to learn
that she already knew almost everything relating to my earlier acquaintance with him. He must therefore have talked to
her about me quite a lot and it indicated that he recalled our

days together with real pleasure and that on her part she regarded it as worth while to remember such things.

She declared amiably that she did not propose to take me on a tour of inspection of the house and the estate because I could see everything that interested me when we rode out in the ordinary way and on the many occasions that she hoped I would now ride over from Unwar as her guest, which she now invited me to be whenever I pleased.

She then reproached the Major for not having visited her for some time and he excused himself, pleading the pressure of work at the harvest and saying in particular that he had not wished to come over without me but that at the same time he had wished to judge first how well or how indifferently I might suit her company.

We then went into a large hall in which we rested for a while after our ride. The Major took advantage of the occasion to produce a writing tablet and ask Brigitta a number of questions, noting down her replies, which were clear, very simply couched and to the point. It was then her turn to ask various questions relating to this or that neighbour, to the business of the moment and to the forthcoming Diet. The discussion gave me an opportunity of observing how earnestly she dealt with such matters and what weight the Major attached to her opinions. When she was uncertain on this or that point she did not hesitate to say so openly and to ask the Major his views.

The Major finally put away his writing tablet and as we were now rested we got up to take a walk on the estate. On the way the talk between them turned to certain alterations she had made on her property since his last visit, and when she spoke of her estate and the things connected with it there was a certain pride and warmth, almost a tenderness, in her tone. She showed us a wooden veranda she had had built on the garden side of the house and she asked the Major whether he thought it would be a good idea to train vines up the pillars, adding that he might well have something of the sort built at his own house as it had proved a very agreeable place to sit in the late autumn sun.

She then led us into the park, which, it appeared, had been just a forest of oak trees ten years previously. Now there were carefully-kept paths laid out through it and banked streams. Deer were grazing there in safety, for in the course of time she had caused a high wall to be built right round it to keep out the wolves. The considerable expense the building of the wall had entailed had been met from the profits of her maize crops and her cattle breeding, both of which she had greatly developed and improved. When the building of the wall had been concluded, huntsmen had thoroughly quartered the whole park to make sure that no wolves— perhaps a mother wolf with her whelps—had been enclosed by the wall, but nothing had been found. Only after that had the deer been established and bred there. It seemed almost as though the deer knew that she was their benefactor, for those we saw on our walk were not in the least timid. As we came near they raised their heads and looked at us with their large velvety eyes but they made no attempt to flee.

Brigitta was obviously very proud of this park and she took great pleasure in showing it to her guests. From there we went on to the pheasantry and as we walked along the wooded paths with little white clouds showing through the oak trees above our heads I took the opportunity of observing her more closely than I had as yet been able to do. Her eyes struck me as even more darkly liquid and more glowing than those of the deer, and perhaps at that moment they were more sparkling than ever because at her side walked a man who understood and appreciated her and knew what she was striving for. Her teeth were very white and her body was still lithe and supple although she was no longer young and she impressed me as having an inexhaustible fund of strength and vitality. As she had expected our visit she was wearing woman's clothes and she had put aside her affairs in order to devote the day to us.

As we walked through the park the talk turned to a great variety of subjects: the future of the country, the raising of the common man and the improvement of his conditions, the tilling and betterment of the soil, the conservancy work for the regulation of the Danube, and the personalities of the prominent men of the country. In this pleasant fashion we went through the greater part of the park, though, as she had said, she made no attempt to show us round on a formal tour of inspection and was interested only in keeping us company.

When we returned to the house it was time to eat. Gustave, her son, appeared at the table. He was bronzed from the sun and the slim, engaging youth looked the picture of health. He had taken his mother's place to supervise the work in the fields that day and now he briefly reported this and that item of interest to her. Otherwise he sat modestly at table with us and listened rather than spoke. In him one could sense a tremendous enthusiasm for the present and an unbounded confidence in the future. Here too, as in the Major's house, it was the custom for the servants attached to the house to eat at the common table and I noticed my old acquaintance Milosch, who acknowledged our previous meeting by greeting me respectfully.

The greater part of the afternoon was then spent inspecting various innovations which the Major had not seen before, and in visits to the gardens and the vineyards.

Towards evening we made ready to ride back to Unwar, and as we were gathering our things together Brigitta reproached the Major with having ridden home one evening from Gömör's estate too lightly clothed for the cool of the evening. He knew very well how treacherous the dewy air of the steppes was at that time of the day so why did he expose himself unnecessarily to its vagaries ? The Major made no attempt to excuse himself but merely replied that in the future he would take better care of himself. I remembered the occasion to which Brigitta referred and I happened to know that when it turned out that her son Gustave had come to Gömör's estate without his Bunda, the Major had insisted that Gustave should take his, declaring, untruthfully, that he had another one to hand in the stables. This time, however, we were both well provided with warm clothing for our return journey in the cool of the evening. Brigitta assured herself that this was really so and stood outside the house with us until we were safely in the saddle wearing our warm jackets. Just before we set off she gave the Major one or two commissions and then she took leave of us amiably and without fuss and went back into the house.

Their conversation throughout the day had been serene and cheerful, but it had seemed to me that when they addressed each other there was a certain inner warmth which neither of them cared to show openly, perhaps regarding themselves as too old for demonstrations of affection. The Major and I rode back together in the moonlight and when I said a few sincere words of admiration for Brigitta which I had been unable to withhold he declared simply:

'My friend, in my life I have often been deeply desired, though whether I was as deeply loved I cannot say, but the society and the regard of that woman have meant more to me than anything else I have ever encountered in this world.'

He spoke calmly and without emotion but with such certainty and deep conviction that it was quite clear that what he said was the simple truth. At that moment, though it is not my nature, I think I envied the Major for this deep friendship and for his good fortune in having been able to settle down so happily, for at that time I had no firm footing anywhere in the world, or anything to which I could cling, except perhaps the stick that accompanied me on my travels through so many countries.

That day, after we had arrived back at Unwar, the Major suggested that I should stay on as his guest throughout the winter as well. He had begun to treat me with still greater intimacy and to open his heart to me, whilst my feelings of regard and affection for him were growing even stronger. I therefore gladly accepted his offer. He then told me that he would like me to take a definite part in the management of his estate, to take over one branch of his activities and to run it entirely. I should have no cause to regret this and in the future it might come in useful. I agreed at once to this suggestion too, and in fact it did prove useful to me. It is largely the Major I have to thank that I now have a household of my own and a loving wife to help me.

Once I had agreed to take a definite and more settled share in the happy and harmonious life he had built up at Unwar I was anxious to do my share to the very best of my ability. I worked hard and enthusiastically and as I became more experienced so I became more capable and was able to be more and more useful. In this way I learnt the profound satisfaction and pleasure of creative activity and my self-respect increased. I realized more and more how much better it is to take up the work at hand and do it thoroughly rather than to idle around from place to place as I had previously been doing on the pretext of gaining experience of life. For the first time I became capable of really sustained and persistent effort.

My life at Unwar was very happy and the time passed almost unnoticeably. I was also a frequent guest at Maroshely, where I came to be looked on almost as a member of the family. At the same time the relationship between Brigitta and the Major became more and more clear to me. There was no question of any secret passion or any feverish desires, and certainly not a trace of the animal magnetism of which I had heard rumours. However, the relationship between the two was certainly unusual and I had never previously encountered anything of the sort. The nature of that relationship was beyond all question what, in the ordinary way and between two people of opposite sexes, we should call love, and yet it did not express itself in the usual way. The Major treated the ageing woman with a tenderness and respect that was reminiscent more of the devotion a man pays to a higher being, and it was clear that it filled her with a profound inner joy. Her happiness showed itself in her face like the blossoming of some late flower and it gave her features an expression of confidence and serenity, and at the same time a radiance that was quite astonishing. She clearly returned his affection and respect in full measure, but in her attitude towards him there was occasionally a trace of anxiety which expressed itself in solicitude for his health and in attention to those minor needs of life, both so typical of a woman when she loves. So much was obvious in the feelings of each for the other, but beyond that there was nothing further in the behaviour or attitude of either.

The Major once confided in me that, at a moment when they had come to talk together of each other in a more intimate fashion than people usually do, they had agreed that they should be united by friendship of the deepest kind, by co-operation towards the same end and by a like striving, but by nothing further. They were both anxious that this calm relationship should remain firmly founded—if possible to the end of their days. They were determined to ask no more of fate, and then there need be no barb, no disappointment. It had been like that between them for a good many years now, he said, and that was how they desired that it should remain.

But man proposes ... It was not long after he had told me this that that fate of which they had both decided to ask no more acted in despite of them and brought about a happening which swiftly and unexpectedly gave matters a very different complexion.

It was already late autumn, in fact winter had really begun, and one day I was riding with the Major along the new road with its double line of poplars. We had proposed to do a little shooting but a thick mist lay over the already frozen steppes. Suddenly as we rode the sound of two shots boomed dully through the mist.

'They were my pistols,' declared the Major. 'I would know the reports anywhere,' and he immediately urged his horse into a furious gallop along the avenue, riding as hard as I have ever seen a man ride. I had a foreboding of evil and I quickly galloped after him towards the spot from where the sound of the shots had come. When I came up with him after a moment or two my eyes saw a spectacle so terrible and yet so thrilling that even now I shudder at it in recollection and my heart beats higher.

By the old gallows tree, where the rush-grown stream flowed past, the Major had come upon the youngster Gustave defending himself against a pack of fierce wolves, but the lad was already clearly tiring. He had killed two wolves

with his pistols and slashed open a third with his blade as
the beast sprang at his horse's head. Now they were standing round him irresolutely for a moment, held off only by
the look of fierce desperation in his eyes. Licking their sla-
vering chops they looked at him and waited their opportunity. A slight movement, anything or nothing, and they
would have sprung at him all together and the boy would
have been lost. But in this critical situation the Major thun-
dered up. He had already dismounted when I arrived and I
was just in time to see him fling himself at the wolves almost as though he were a wild animal himself. I had heard
two more reports and the Major had fired from the saddle,
killing two more wolves. Now I saw his hunting blade flash
left and right amongst the ravening beasts. From his arrival
the whole affair lasted three or four seconds, no more. I had
just time to empty my hunting piece into the pack and they
were gone, swallowed up by the thick mist all around, and
all that was left of them was the dead bodies of those that
had been killed.

'Reload,' shouted the Major. 'They'll attack again.' He
recovered his own pistol, a double-barrelled model, and
rammed home the cartridges. Gustave and I also reload-
ed. No sooner had we done so and were waiting there for
a moment or so listening than we heard the soft footfall of
wolves from beyond the gallows tree. The famished but in-
timidated brutes had now surrounded us. At any moment
they would attack again. When they are not driven on by
hunger, as they were now, wolves are cowardly creatures
and more likely to flee than to attack. However, we were
not equipped for wolf hunting and the wretched all-pervad-
ing mist made it impossible to see very far so we decided to
get back to the house. We mounted and set our horses into a
gallop. The frightened beasts needed no urging and they galloped along madly and more than once as we rode I caught
a glimpse of a grey shadow loping along silently beside us
in the mist. The wolves were tracking us relentlessly and
we had to be on our guard the whole time. Once the Major discharged his pistol to the left, but it was impossible to

see whether he hit his mark and there was no time for talk. Finally we reached the park gates and the dogs which had been waiting there rushed out and chased after the wolves. A moment later we heard angry howling behind us and then it died away in the distance as the wolves fled from the dogs over the steppes.

'To horse all of you,' shouted the Major to his men as they ran up. 'Let the wolfhounds loose. I don't want my dogs to come to any harm. Rouse the neighbourhood and set the hunt going. Hunt them as long as you please. A double reward for every dead wolf except those lying near the gallows tree, for we killed them ourselves. One of the pistols I gave Gustave last year must be lying around there somewhere. I see he had only one and the other holster is empty. See if you can find the other pistol.'

Then the Major turned to me.

'It's five years since wolves ventured so close to the house,' he said. 'We were beginning to feel fairly secure. It looks as though there's going to be a hard winter. It must already have set in to the north to bring them so far south so early in the season.'

The men had rushed off to carry out their master's orders, and in less time than I would have believed possible a party of eager men was on horseback accompanied by a pack of those great shaggy dogs which are so typical of the Hungarian pusta and so necessary to the men who live and work on it. They made arrangements for rousing the neighbourhood and then they set off on a hunt which could last a week, a fortnight, and even longer.

Without dismounting we sat there and watched the rapid preparations, but as we finally turned away from the outbuildings and made our way towards the house we observed that Gustave was faint from a wound he had received. As we turned in under the archway which led to the living quarters he suffered a fit of giddiness and almost fell from his horse. One of the servants caught him and helped him from the saddle and then we saw that the saddle and the flanks of the horse were stained with blood.

We carried the lad into one of the rooms on the garden floor and the Major ordered a bed to be prepared and a fire lit. The Major gently removed the boy's clothing and examined the wound. It proved to be a bite in the thigh; nothing very dangerous, but the loss of blood and the excitement had weakened the lad, who was now fighting against the faintness it induced. He was then made as comfortable as possible in bed and the local doctor was sent for whilst another servant rode over to Maroshely to let Brigitta know what had happened. In the meantime the Major remained by the boy's bedside and did his best for him until the doctor arrived. After examining the patient the doctor declared that there was no danger. All the boy needed was a stimulant. Far from being serious, the loss of blood was a good thing: it would help to counteract the inflammation that so often set in after such bites. The chief trouble was the shock and excitement, but a day or two in bed would put the boy right and dispose of any feverishness. It wouldn't be long before he was on his feet again.

We were all very much relieved to hear this good report and the doctor then left with our warm thanks, for there was not one of us in the house who was not deeply attached to the lad.

Towards evening Brigitta appeared, and in her usual thorough and conscientious fashion she was not satisfied until she had examined her son very carefully to make quite certain that there was nothing else wrong with him beyond the bite. When she had finished her examination she stayed by her son's bedside and gave him the medicine the doctor had prescribed. A second bed was quickly made up for her in the same room and there she spent the night. The next morning she was once again sitting by the boy's bedside and listening to his breathing. It was perfectly regular and he was sleeping soundly and peacefully.

And then something happened that made an ineradicable impression on me. I can still see the scene clearly before my eyes. I had come down early in order to inquire how the patient was doing and I had gone into the room adjoining the sick-room. The latter, as I have already said, gave on to the garden. The mist had gone and a red winter's sun was shining into the room through the leafless branches of the trees in the garden. The Major was also in the room with me and he stood at the window and seemed to be looking out into the garden. I could see through the open door into the sick-room where the early-morning light had been subdued a little by light curtains drawn over the windows. Brigitta was sitting by the bed and looking closely at her son. Suddenly she gave a sigh of relief and as I looked at her I glimpsed the light of happy love and devotion in her eyes as she saw that the boy had woken up out of his long sleep and was looking around serenely.

Then I heard a slight sound, almost like a stifled groan, from where the Major had been standing and I looked round. He had half turned back into the room and I saw that there were tears in his eyes. I went towards him, anxiously asking if anything were wrong.

'I have no child,' he said softly.

Brigitta's hearing was very keen and she must have heard the half-whispered words, for at that moment she appeared in the doorway. She looked a little uncertainly at my friend and then with an expression I cannot describe, as though she wanted to say something and hardly dared, she said simply:

'Stephen.'

The Major turned towards her and they looked at each other wordlessly for a moment, but no more than a moment. Then he strode resolutely towards her and they were in each other's arms. She held him tightly to her and I heard him utter a low sound, and this time there was no room for doubt: it was a sob. At that she embraced him even more closely.

'We shall never part again, Brigitta,' I heard him say. 'Neither now nor ever.'

'Never, Stephen,' she replied fervently. 'Never.'

I was very ill at ease at being present at such an intimate moment and I moved silently towards the door, but she raised her hand.

'Don't go, my friend,' she said. 'Stay here.'

The serious, high-minded woman had been weeping with her head on my friend's shoulder. Her eyes were still wet with tears as she looked at me and her face was radiant with indescribable beauty, for on it there was forgiveness, the most beautiful quality we poor miserable creatures here below can aspire to. At the sight my own feelings were deeply moved.

'My poor wife,' exclaimed the Major. 'For fifteen long years I have had to do without you, and for fifteen years you were sacrificed.'

She smiled gently up at him.

'I was at fault,' she said softly. 'Forgive me, Stephen. It was the sin of pride. But I had no conception of how good you are. And, after all, the thing was quite natural. We are all drawn irresistibly by what is beautiful.'

He put his hand over her lips.

'How can you say such a thing, Brigitta! Yes, it is true, we are all attracted by the beautiful, but I had to wander all over the world before I learnt that it was in our own hearts and that I had abandoned it in the one heart that loved me loyally and steadfastly, a heart I thought I had lost for ever but which still went with me through all those years and all those many countries. Brigitta, my wife and the mother of my child, you were always with me, by day and by night.'

'Yes, I was not lost to you,' she replied. 'But I have spent sad and regretful years. How good you are, Stephen! Now that I know you, how good you are!'

And they embraced again as though they could never embrace enough, as though they could still hardly believe in the good fortune that had come to them again. They were like two people from whom a great burden has been suddenly lifted. Once again the world stood open to them. They were happy as children are happy, and at that moment they were as innocent as children, for the highest bloom of love, and only the highest form of love, is forgiveness, and therefore man will always find it in God and in a mother. Great hearts will forgive again and again; poor creatures never.

Husband and wife had forgotten my presence again and they now turned to the sick-room where Gustave lay in bed, half-guessing what had happened and eagerly awaiting their coming.

'Gustave! Gustave!' exclaimed Brigitta as they entered the room. 'It was your father all the time and you did not know it.'

Deeply moved at what I had seen and heard I now took the opportunity of going unobtrusively out into the garden. For the first time in my life I truly realized what a noble thing the love of husband and wife is and I counted myself wretched that up to then all I had known of love was the dark, smouldering flame of passion.

I stayed away from the house for some time and when I finally returned everything was calm and serene and all emotional tension had been resolved. Happy and bustling activity now filled the rooms like cheerful sunshine after a storm. I was received with open arms as a dear witness of the joyful thing that had taken place. Once they had discovered that in their preoccupation with each other I had gone they had searched for me everywhere. Gradually I learned everything that had happened then and before.

Some of it I learned at once there and then in their elation; the rest I learned in the days that followed until I was able to piece together all the details and set down my story.

My old friend the Major was thus Stephen Murai. After leaving his wife he had called himself Stephen Bathori, which was his family name on the distaff side, and that was the name under which I had always known him. He had won the rank of Major in Spain, and everyone had always referred to him by it. He had travelled all over Europe under the name of Bathori and when he finally went to his neglected estate at Unwar, where no one knew him and to which he seemed drawn by some inner necessity, it was as Stephen Bathori. Although no one on his own estate there knew him, or had ever seen him there, he knew that he would be the neighbour of his wife Brigitta. But even after he had settled in Unwar he did not visit her on the estate at Maroshely she was managing so efficiently, and it was not until he heard the news of her serious illness that he did so. But then he mounted his horse and rode over at once. Her temperature was so high when he arrived that she was already wandering and she did not recognize him. After that he remained day and night at Maroshely and tended her devotedly until she recovered.

It was then that, deeply moved by their first meeting after so many years, and still deeply attached to each other by a love that had never really ceased, but also a little frightened at the thought of their future, for they were still uncertain of each other and both feared that something might again happen to separate them, they made the strange pact by which they should remain no more than firm friends. For years they had both strictly respected it and neither of them had dared to call it into question—until fate suddenly struck at both of them through their son Gustave. Their common anxiety for what they both loved so deeply then threw them into each other's arms and brought them together once again in the more natural and more beautiful relationship of the married couple and dissipated all doubts and all fears.

After a fortnight the news was made known in the neighbourhood and well-wishers began to come in from near and far to present their congratulations.

I remained with them throughout the winter, but at Maroshely, to which they now all moved. It was the Major's firm intention never to take his wife away from the little world she had built up for herself in his absence. Perhaps the most obviously delighted and happy of them all was Gustave. He had always been deeply attached to the Major and with the earnest and burning enthusiasm of youth he had always declared him to be the finest man on God's earth. And now the man he had almost worshipped proved to be his father.

That winter I watched two hearts grow more closely together than ever before in a splendid if belated blossoming of married happiness.

I will never forget any of them as long as I live.

But when spring came again I resumed my old German travelling garb, took my stout German stick and turned my steps in the direction of my own Fatherland once again. On my way I visited the grave of the lovely Gabrielle, who had died twelve years previously in the full bloom of all her youthful beauty. Two white lilies lay on the marble slab of her grave.

With melancholy but gentle thoughts I continued my journey and soon I was across the Leitha and in the distance I could see the blue haze that I knew to be the mountains of my own dear Fatherland.

Contents

Printed in the United States
37551LVS00003B/13

9 781595 690142